THE BLOOD TRAIL
THE COMPLETE CASES OF MORTON
& McGARVEY, VOLUME 2

THE BLOOD TRAIL

THE COMPLETE CASES OF
MORTON & McGARVEY,
VOLUME 2

DONALD BARR CHIDSEY

COVER BY
C.C. BEALL

POPULAR PUBLICATIONS · 2023

TABLE OF CONTENTS

MURDER TO ORDER

The Trail of the Mysterious .45 Led Morton
and McGarvey Through Walls of Steel to
the Sinister Cache of a Murder Dealer

1

SMUGGLERS OF DEATH

McGARVEY WAS BORED. The millionaires and racketeers, the rich widows and divorcees, the gamblers, gigolos, invalids, gunmen, sportsmen, artists, crooks, all had gone home; and things were very quiet. McGarvey always was bored when things were that way. He was young and enormous and maybe not very bright.

When the telephone rang he was tilted far back in a chair glowering at the ceiling; his feet were on the desk.

Across that desk was Morton, trim and precise; quiet and methodical. Morton, more than twice as old as his partner, didn't like things to go wrong. He was past the age when he enjoyed excitement.

McGarvey answered the phone. Morton hadn't even moved.

"Yeah?... Yeah, this is him...."

His feet came down, the front legs of his chair hit the floor, his mouth fell open, his eyes bulged. Morton, still without moving his head, looked at him from under fluffy gray eyebrows.

"At Stake's, you say?... Wait a minute? Who is this?"

Light as a gymnast, for all his bulk, he bounded away from desk and chair. He didn't even reach for his coat. Morton, without seeming to hurry, was right after him.

McGarvey called, "Stick-up at Stake's, Flagler Street! Flash it! At Stake's!"

He would have used the car, but Morton said:

"Run it! Quicker!"

McGarvey swerved, sprang between two automobiles, pulling his gun. Brakes shrieked. Morton ran between two other automobiles.

Long-legged McGarvey got there first. He whammed open a pair of doors, saw two clerks behind a counter on the left, two men facing them with pistols. One of the clerks screamed, stiffened, toppled sideways. The nearest gunman swung on his heel, shooting. McGarvey charged him, firing three times. The bandit gave a little jump backward on his heels. He started to fall, and his right elbow struck the counter as he squeezed the gun twice more. McGarvey was over him even before he hit the floor, and was clouting him above the ear with his pistol.

The second bandit, a little man, bent low and sprinted for the doors, which still were swinging from the force of McGarvey's push. He half turned, fired once in the general direction of McGarvey, then started again for the sidewalk. His belly hit the point of a pistol so hard that it almost knocked him out. He went "Aw-oof" and his knees wobbled.

"Drop it," Morton sighed.

A beautiful piece of work. The whole business, from start to finish, had not taken more than eight minutes.

To be sure, the lookout-driver escaped. The cop on the beat had been told, half a block away, that Stake's was being stuck up, and at the same time he had seen Morton and McGarvey charging along the opposite sidewalk. He had

*Whitey's fall spun
McGarvey around.
He jerked out his
gun as he turned.*

run after them. Had he thought fast enough he could have
headed off the man in the getaway car; but that car started
simultaneously with the crashing of the big show window
by a bullet intended for McGarvey, so it is little wonder
that the uniformed man didn't stop to scrutinize it.

However, Morton, within twenty-five minutes, rounded
up no less than ten persons who had seen the driver. By
the following afternoon the dead man and the prisoner
had been identified by means of fingerprint classification
telegraphed to New York, and copies of the likenesses of
five associates of these men were on the way to Florida by
airplane. That night the getaway car was found abandoned
in Fort Lauderdale; it had been stolen in Coral Gables less
than an hour before the hold-up. Next morning the rogues'
gallery pictures arrived from New York and eight of the

ten persons who had seen the missing man unhesitatingly picked his picture from the five. What's more, each of them picked the same picture.

A general alarm was sent out for Maurice "Whitey" Wilson.

Yes, it was a beautiful piece of work. And once again Florida, in the form of resolutions, private conversations, public speeches, votes of gratitude and letters to editors was shouting the praises of an iron-gray detective veteran and his young partner.

McGARVEY BASKED IN it, grinning. He was only a kid and glory meant a lot to him. But bland and patient Morton worked right through it all—worked tirelessly, ploddingly, silently, at the sort of work good cops have to do, the work for which they get no publicity. So that when, a week later, New York long-distanced that they had picked up Whitey Wilson and were holding him for extradition, Morton had a long report to make.

"Wilson was clear, but both the others were parole boys out of Sing Sing. And all three of them had records a mile long. They probably wouldn't have dared come down here in the season while we had New York dicks visiting us here who might have spotted them."

Montgomery said: "Somebody ought to've seen them on the way down."

"Somebody did. The day before the hold-up they passed through Jacksonville on the Havana Limited, in a drawing room. They had to wait over for a while in Jacksonville, of course, and while they were there Wes Haviland and Joey Birch went through the train on a general-principles snooping tour. Wes saw Wilson stick his head out for some air, so he and Joey barged in and did a little asking. They didn't pinch any of the three of 'em because, as far as they knew, none of them was wanted for anything. But they did frisk them and go through their baggage."

"But those guys had—"

"I know. The two in the store each had a .45 automatic and another .45 automatic was found in the car. But they didn't have those when they went through Jacksonville. Birch and Wes Haviland told me so, over the phone yesterday. And they couldn't have got the guns at West Palm Beach, which is the only other place the train stopped. The West Palm Beach cops say only four people got off there, and nobody got on. Not one of these boys had any connections here, as far as we know, and yet they had their guns waiting for them. They had Stake's cased, and they were walking in there a few hours after they'd arrived in Miami.

"Not only that, but they had time to make an enemy here. Because that phone call wasn't any report from a citizen—it was a tip. The guy, whoever he was, said he saw stick-up men going into Stake's, but as a matter of fact those men had just got inside there, from what the clerks say, when Garv and I arrived. The guy who telephoned didn't see any stick-up, but he knew there was going to be one, and he knew where, and exactly when.

"Another thing." He handed Captain Montgomery a list of numbers sent out by the Bureau of Investigation, Department of Justice, Washington, D.C. The numbers were those of pistols stolen from national guard armories in and around New York City. "The three with 'x's' next to them are the three we got from this job. The others, with checks next to them are guns we've confiscated here

within the past three months. In five different jobs here
army pistols have been used, nine of them altogether. We're
absolutely certain it wasn't one gang that pulled all those
jobs. But still they all had the same kind of guns, swiped
from the same places."

Montgomery studied the list, frowning. He had learned
to depend upon Wentworth L. Morton; but he never did
know, nor did anybody else, what was in Morton's mind
at a given time.

Montgomery asked: "Well, what do you make of it?"

"Only that it might be a good idea if I had a chance to
talk things over with Centre Street, and also maybe with
the federals in New York. It might get us somewhere. Can't
tell. So why not me and McGarvey going up to bring back
this Whitey Wilson?"

The captain shook his head.

"Wilson's nothing but a punk, according to New York."

"Take it this way," Morton said. "The papers are all playing up Garv and me right now, and it would look like a
natural thing if we should be sent to bring this guy back
and clean up the whole case."

"Be like using a couple of sledge hammers to swat a
mosquito with. And it isn't only that… After all, extradition's a sheriff's office matter."

"Sure, I know that. But I also know that you've got the
pull to arrange it. And what the hell? I'm a deputy, besides
being a city detective, ain't I? Garv isn't, but we can swear
him in for the occasion."

Morton rose.

"Even a sledge hammer," he pointed out, "needs a vacation now and then. It'll do me good, and it'll do the kid good too."

"Well…" said Montgomery.

PEOPLE WHO HAD only heard about them, or read about them, and didn't know them personally, probably thought of Morton and McGarvey as a couple of stone-faced super-sleuths with beetling brows, bloodless lips, camera eyes, hearts of ice and the infallible instinct of bloodhounds. As a matter of fact, neither of them looked much like a detective. Morton was too old, too staid, and McGarvey was much too young and noisy. Certainly newspaper readers would not have recognized them on the *Okeechobee*.

Grizzled Morton sat all day in the smoking saloon, soundlessly playing solitaire. He sometimes smoked a cigarette, or, if somebody gave him one, a cigar. He drank beer tirelessly. Each time he'd take a drink he carefully laid down his cards, and afterward he would stare thoughtfully for a moment at the remaining beer, or at the bottom of the stein, and then, sighing, resume his game; When casual acquaintances or total strangers, in passing, playfully warned him against cheating, he would nod politely but without a smile. He looked absentminded and a little tired.

But for McGarvey this trip was a holiday. McGarvey, twenty-three years old, never had been further north than Savannah, Georgia; further south than Key West; further west than Tallahassee; further east than he could swim off Miami Beach—which was pretty far east at that, for he was a powerful swimmer.

Everything thrilled him. Before they were out of Miami harbor he had climbed all over the ship, talked with sailors, made acquaintances among the male passengers—he was

shy of women, old or young—and twice been ordered off
the bridge. Before they turned into the St. John's River, for
the stop at Jacksonville, he had obtained permission from
the chief engineer to go below and gape at the *Okeechobee's*
not remarkable engines. At Charleston, where Morton
spent the shore hours gravely chatting with some cronies
at police headquarters, McGarvey was roaming along the
waterfront, buying buttonholes in Meeringhouse Square,
reading the plates attached to cannons in the parks, and
gazing in awe at the breathlessly aristocratic Battery
mansions. Long before Cape May was raised he was hanging over the rail scanning the horizon.

"Not looking for porpoises, are you?"

McGarvey turned, feeling a bit foolish. He knew this
tall, amiable man in tweeds. Name was Hedbirn. Arthur
Hedbirn. A New Yorker, middle-aged and apparently
prosperous. McGarvey liked him. He liked to talk with
him, stroll around the deck with him. But Hedbirn was
so smooth a dresser, so finished a conversationalist, that
the crude McGarvey always felt awkward in his presence.

"I was just wondering when we'll sight land."

"It won't be over there," Hedbirn said. "That's east, the
way you're looking."

"Oh."

"Shall we go over to the other side?"

SO THEY LEANED against the rail on the other side, and
they talked of this and that. McGarvey admitted that it
was his first visit to New York.

"My partner and me are coming up to get this little runt
Wilson that drove the car those two stick-up guys used in
that jewelry store job in Miami last week."

Hedbirn said, opening his eyes wide: "Oh, you're *that* McGarvey?"

"Well, yes."

"Oh, I read about that! In Charleston. I got on at Charleston, you know. But I'd read about you and Sergeant Morton before. You're the son of the Frank McGarvey who was killed fighting some gangsters in a roadhouse down there a year or so ago, aren't you? He and Morton were partners?"

"Well, yes. Mort and the old man were pretty close too, and I guess that's the only reason they boosted me out of harness after the old man got killed. It was just being sentimental, I guess. Mort doesn't really need a partner. He's got more brains than all the rest of them down there put together. He's one swell detective, Mort is!"

"Yes, so I've always heard." Not only was Hedbirn tall, but his face was the face of a tall man. It was a sharp face, but benign; a fatherly sort of face, pale and thin and unworldly. He was well dressed, and comfortably dressed too, but given a cowl and a severe haircut he could have posed as a picture book monk. Now he looked sideways at McGarvey. "In fact," he said, "I've read as much about this Morton as about you or your father."

It embarrassed McGarvey, who tried to change the subject.

"You're an art dealer, aren't you?"

"Yes. Antiques chiefly."

"I don't know much about art."

Hedbirn laughed. "Well, if it comes to that, I don't know much about police work. But I've always thought it must be fascinating."

"It's fun, sometimes." New Jersey still failed to appear on the horizon, and McGarvey simply couldn't resist the temptation to boast about his partner. He was incalculably proud of Morton. "This job of coming up to New York to get a no-account little squirt like Wilson," he confided, "that isn't the sort of thing Mort would be interested in, ordinarily."

"Just a kind of vacation for him?"

"Well, no. Not exactly. Mort never does take vacations. No, there's more to it than that," McGarvey said mysteriously. "There's a reason why we want to take Wilson back ourselves. But of course I can't tell you about that."

"Oh, naturally! I wouldn't expect you to!"

There was a long silence while McGarvey tried to think of something intelligent to say about art or antiques. And still no sign of New Jersey.

Hedbirn said: "But I suppose it would be all right to ask you to point out some of the more important officials at the dock?"

"What officials?"

"Why, the police officials. Won't the New York police department send a delegation or something down to the dock to meet you?"

For a horrified instant McGarvey wondered whether he was being kidded. He looked sharply at Hedbirn. But Hedbirn seemed in earnest.

"Hell, no! I guess the cops in a place like New York got something better to do with their time. No, there won't be anybody there. We'll just go to headquarters and identify ourselves and make arrangements to take over the prisoner, and then go back by train. The extradition's been fixed up and all that."

"I see," said Hedbirn.

"There won't be anything to it," McGarvey said, and added significantly: "That is, on the surface."

"I see."

2

HOLD-UP AT SEA

THAT AFTERNOON McGARVEY went into the smoking room.

"We're going to be late. Won't get in till almost ten tonight."

Morton, placing a red seven on a black eight, said: "Waiter! Bring me a beer!" He knew better than to offer McGarvey one.

"I'll be glad to get in, at that. It's been pretty slow.

"Made any friends?"

"A few. One guy I was talking to this morning asked me if the New York cops would have a delegation down at the dock to greet us. I mean, you and me. I told him I didn't think so. He meant it, too!" McGarvey rose. "Dinner bell rang twenty minutes ago."

"I'll be going down," said Morton, putting a black six on the red seven, "as soon as I've finished this game."

"I don't see how you can just sit there playing that crazy solitaire all the time!" McGarvey started for the deck below. "Don't you even want to come out and see the lights of Sandy Hook?"

"I've seen them before," said Morton.

McGarvey, disgusted, was half-way to the door when the shot sounded.

He stopped, jerked his shoulders back, reached for his gun. Morton's head went up. They were motionless for a moment.

Aside from these two, and the steward behind the little service bar, the smoking room was deserted. Indeed, the whole ship seemed deserted. The *Okeechobee* was carrying less than half her capacity of passengers, and most of these at the time were in the dining room or in their separate cabins, packing.

The shot had seemed to come from the corridor to the right, forward of the smoking saloon. A moment later a door slammed. Then there was a sound of something metallic hitting the deck outside. Then somebody shouting: "Help! Help! I'm being robbed!"

Once a cop always a cop, anywhere and at all times. McGarvey and Morton had no authority aboard the *Okeechobee*, but they sprang as one man for the door, dashed past a stair well, down the corridor. In front of the fourth door a tall, white-haired man waved his arms.

"Somebody tried to shoot me!"

McGarvey gasped: "Hello, Mr. Hedbirn! Me, McGarvey! Who was it?"

"I don't know. I was just going into my room, and before I had a chance to snap on the light somebody stuck something into my ribs and told me to put up my hands. I was terrified! I guess I must have moved or something—I don't remember—and he must have thought I was resisting him. Anyway, the next thing I knew a gun went off, and somebody ran down the hall."

"You hurt?"

"No. At least, I guess not. I don't seem to be."

Morton had run down the hall, wriggling around people who were popping out of staterooms. He dodged through a door to the deck, looked right and left. A short distance away, in the water gutter at the base of the rail, was a large black automatic pistol. Morton looked at the pistol, looked at the rail, picked up the pistol with two fingers. He sniffed the muzzle. By this time McGarvey was at his shoulder.

"Colt's P.F.A. Mfg. Co., Hartford, Ct.," Morton read. And then: "United States Property."

They went back to Hedbirn's stateroom. There, while McGarvey asked questions, Morton went over the pistol with white powder.

"What did this guy look like, Mr. Hedbirn?"

"I don't know! I never really saw him!"

"You know anybody who'd want to shoot you?"

"Why, of course not!"

"Know any reason why any crook should go after you?"

"No, except that sometimes I have miniatures and things like that, that are worth quite a bit. In fact, I've got some on this trip, that I bought in Charleston. But they're locked up in the purser's safe."

Morton had abandoned the pistol and was examining the stateroom. In the support of the electric fan, fastened to a wall, he found a sharp groove. He found a somewhat similar mark, a little higher, on a steampipe.

"Did some richochetting," he surmised.

Eventually he found the bullet itself, embedded in the woodwork of the ceiling. He dug it out.

"Lands and grooves all crushed. Not much good to

a ballistics man." He handed it to the purser, who, with several other ship's officers, was crowded in the doorway. "Better lock it up, along with the gun."

McGarvey blurted: "What're you going to do now, Mort?"

"Me?" said Morton. "Going downstairs and get something to eat."

AFTER DINNER, WITH some lowering of dignity, the captain went to Morton instead of asking Morton to come to him; and with the captain were the first officer, the purser, and McGarvey. Morton was in the smoking saloon. He seemed glum. But it was always hard to tell how Morton felt about anything.

"It's none of my business," he said. "Garv here seems to like this guy, Hedbirn, and if he wants to help him that's his lookout. But me, I'm a Dade County deputy sheriff, and this is the high seas."

The captain expostulated: "But you're a trained detective! If you were the only physician around when somebody was hurt in an accident, you certainly wouldn't refuse to help them just because they weren't one of your regular patients? Here we've got a dangerous criminal on board, and we're going to dock soon, and we don't know what to do about it. Won't you at least make some suggestion?"

"Sure. I suggest what I did before, that you turn the whole thing over to the federals. It's their job."

"We've already radioed to the New York police."

"All right. They'll notify the federals."

"But we'd like to have something definite to report! We can't delay. We're late now. You must have seen practically all the passengers, Mr. Morton. There aren't many of them, this trip. Do any of them look like criminals to you?"

Morton said: "Oh, one of them's an assault and battery artist, and maybe a gunman for all I know. Name's Walkely. Slim Walkely."

"But why didn't you report this the moment you recognized him? Good Lord! Here we've been making a whole trip with a known criminal aboard and we never even knew it!"

Now for the first time Morton showed a trace of impatience.

"You make a lot of trips with criminals on board and never know it, Captain. Trouble is, a lot of you fellows think a gangster or a crook is somebody with a dirty cap and a turtle neck sweater that leans against lamp posts. Or else a slick foreigner with a black velour hat and diamonds all over him. Why, man, there are criminals all around you! You walk the streets with them, you buy things in stores from them, you sit next to them at dinner. I don't mean just petty sneak thieves either. I mean big shots and killers. They're everywhere! And they have offices and play golf and travel and dance at country clubs just like anybody else. Why should I run to you when I happen to see a criminal on board? The wonder of it is that there's only one. On the average trip like this I'll bet I could spot at least three for you. Twice that many in the middle of the season. Besides, what can you do about Walkely? He's not wanted for anything, anywhere, as far as I know. He's got a perfect right to be here. I can't run him in for just being here."

"Well—I suppose— But you might at least *question* him!"

"I have, already. Just after dinner."

"What did he say?"

"Exactly what you'd expect him to say: That he never even heard of Hedbirn and wasn't anywhere near that corridor at that time; that he didn't have any stolen property in his stateroom or on his person, and that if I didn't believe him I could go ahead and search. Which I did. And found nothing."

"But can this man prove where he was at the time?"

"He doesn't have to. That's up to you. Only from what I know of Slim Walkely he wouldn't try to stick up a guy who probably wouldn't have anything on him anyway, and aboard a ship where he's one of the passengers and sure to be suspected. Slim's no intellectual genius, but he's not as dumb as all that."

Morton frowned a little, spread his palms.

"All I can suggest is that as soon as we dock you tell the cops what happened and point out Walkely to them—or I'll do that part, if you want me to—and hand over the gun."

McGARVEY CRIED: "WHOEVER pulled this job ran out on the deck there and tried to throw the gun overboard afterward. But it hit the top of the rail and fell back. You can see the mark there."

Morton, not heeding, went on: "Tell 'em I dusted the gun and found nothing. Also I checked its serial number and found out that its one of sixty-five or seventy stolen from an armory in the Bronx several months ago. Government property. Which is all the more reason why the federals will be interested. And while I think of it, turn that slug over to them at the same time, and suggest that they have it weighed."

"Have it weighed? What for?"

Morton shrugged.

"Just a hunch."

The *Okeechobee*, a not important ship, a modest, humble, indeed almost a forgotten ship, returning after a routine run in the off-season, must have been astounded at the officialdom which ascended to her deck as soon as the planks were out. A coastwise vessel, she was not accustomed to customs and public health and immigration officers; and certainly she never had expected, as she neared the end of her unexciting career, to be the scene of such bustle and fuss.

The first officer had framed the radiogram to Centre Street, and some of his own perturbation—he was a quiet fellow, given to checkers, and rubbers, and mouth washes—must have seeped into it. Centre Street wasn't sure, after perusal of that message, what it was all about. It might have been a riot. There was no time for further messages; the *Okeechobee* already was plodding through quarantine; so Centre Street played safe.

Four Department of Justice agents attached to the New York office and seven appropriately burly plainclothes-men of the city's force pounded up the gangplank before any passenger was permitted to descend; while on the deck below, strategically placed, were no less than twelve uniformed patrolmen, some of them carrying automatic rifles.

Whatever the *Okeechobee* might have felt, Slim Walkely was calm. Walkely had been nicknamed "Slim" in an earlier day. Now he was plump and well tanned, slow-moving, with a smile for everybody. He wore a polo coat, a camel's hair cap, and, unexpectedly, cloth-topped shoes. There was nothing bold about him, but neither was there anything furtive. He nodded to three of the city detectives, greeted them like old friends.

Hedbirn was confronted with this suspect, and protested again that he could not possibly identify the man who had fired at him.

"I never saw the fellow! Anyway, I was so scared that even if I had seen him I'm sure I wouldn't be able to give a decent description."

"It wasn't me," Walkely said. "I don't do things like that. I'm just a fur cutter now."

"I think it might be a good idea," Lieutenant Burns said, "if we took you to a precinct house and asked you a few questions, anyway."

Walkely shrugged, looked pained.

"All I got to say is, you guys certainly got a funny way of doing business. But I suppose I might as well go with you."

"Yeah," Burns said. "I suppose you might as well."

Hedbirn was asked once more to repeat his story. He was badly flustered, and the cops were kind and didn't detain him. McGarvey, at Hedbirn's own request, escorted him to a taxicab.

"There's nothing to be frightened about. It's just that the gun this guy Walkely used, if it was Walkely, happens to be one that was stolen from a national guard armory, and naturally the police are anxious to find out who's peddling those guns."

"It seems horrible," Hedbirn said, "to think that the

United States army, which is meant for our protection, is all the time supplying pistols to the hoodlums and gangsters."

"It certainly does," McGarvey agreed. "More than half the real trouble we had down in Miami this last season was caused by no-accounts who were able to make a big show because somebody'd sold them Colts that were meant for the soldiers. I wish they'd guard their damn armories better up here!"

From the taxicab Hedbirn said: "I can't thank you enough, Mr. McGarvey. All this may be an every day matter to you, but it's really shaken me sadly. I won't get a wink of sleep tonight."

"Forget it. Glad to've been some help."

"Will you be in the city long?"

"No, we're starting back tomorrow night."

"Too bad. I was going to ask you to drop in on me at the Hotel Besser, if you had the chance. I'd like to show you some of my antiques."

"Certainly sorry I won't be able to. There's a lot of things in this town I'd like to see, if it come to that. But— Oh, well!"

Morton didn't seem interested in the business. He wanted to get to a hotel and call it a night. Burns asked him if he wouldn't care to be in on the questioning of Walkely, but Morton shook his head. The federal men, obviously not popular with the city detectives, took charge of the gun and the slug.

On the way uptown McGarvey asked his partner why he'd been so gruff.

"I'm tired," Morton answered. "Lord, can't a guy get tired?"

McGarvey himself might have been tired, but he wouldn't admit it. Though it was almost midnight when at last they checked into a hotel, McGarvey couldn't think of sleeping. He went outside, all aquiver with eagerness, and for almost three hours he wandered around Times and Longacre Squares, gaping unabashed at the bright lights and the big buildings. Morton was sound asleep when he returned.

3

MCGARVEY *VERSUS* THE N.Y. POLICE FORCE

IN HEADQUARTERS NEXT morning McGarvey thrilled
at the attention with which they were received. He was no
fool: he knew that the fuss was not being made about *him*,
but about his partner; but this very fact made him thrill the
more. It did his heart good to see high officials of the greatest police department in the world recognize Wentworth
L. Morton, hail him, pump his hand. Morton, of course,
had been in Centre Street many times, and had gained an
even closer acquaintanceship with New York police poten-
tates through their own visits to Miami.

No less a personage than Deputy Commissioner Martin
was their host.

"If you boys want to take in the line-up you've got just
about time. It's five minutes to nine now. Do you want to
go?"

The line-up! Rapture! Young McGarvey nodded eagerly,
and Morton also nodded. Martin called in a stringy, chalky
man in plainclothes, a man with purple-gray eyes and a
blue chin.

"This is Sergeant Beddicker, boys. Sergeant, will you
take Mr. Morton and Mr. McGarvey to the line-up, and

afterward show them around." And as they were going out
through the large blue octagonal reception room Martin
called: "Lunch with me, Mort, when you're through?"

"Sure," said Morton.

So they sat and watched the punks and pimps and
panhandlers, the loft burglars, the rollers, the bums and
grifters, the confidence men, the Communists, the murderers, the stick-up boys, and all the other sweepings of a
New York night parade across a platform blazing with
light, and take their hats off and put them on again, and
stand in front of a bold measuring stick and answer questions into a microphone, while several hundred detectives
in the dim gymnasium stared and grunted and chuckled
and glowered, according to their respective temperaments
and experiences.

They saw, among others, Archie "Slim" Walkely. He did
look flustered. He had been on this platform many times.

"This bozo," the inspector at the high desk said into his
microphone, "has been up the river twice for assault and
once for larceny, and he's still walking around looking for
trouble."

"Jake," Walkely said earnestly, "trouble is exactly what I
ain't looking for any more. I'm through with that."

"Slim," said the inspector, "you're a liar. This bozo," the
inspector went on, "was picked up when he came in on a
boat from Florida last night, and he's suspected of trying
to pull a holdup there, just before she docked. He tried to
throw his gun overboard."

"Jake, I never saw that gun in my life."

"Yeah! Now here's the point: That gun was one of the
ones stolen from the armory up Grand Concourse two

months or so ago. Those guns have been showing up all over the country ever since, along with a lot of others that were stolen from other armories around here. Plenty of them were picked up in Florida. Well, Slim here just came back from Florida."

"Jake, I'm a fur cutter. That's all I am."

"Stop making speeches! This bozo knows something about where those guns are being dealt out, but he won't crack open for us—which is going to make it all the tougher for you, Slim, when we do get something on you! The ring that's been passing out those guns is doing more to encourage organized crime in this country than anything else I can think of, and the federals are working on it night and day. It's right here in the city somewheres and the commissioner would certainly like to see the department here mop it up. Even if they did it before the federals got anywhere on the case the commissioner wouldn't mind."

A Negro who had used a bottle on somebody's skull early that morning was ushered up the steps and stood blinking in the lights.

"Jake, are you through with me, please?" Walkely pleaded.

"Yes! Go wan! Go back and cut some more fur! And if I was you I'd keep away from those gun-runners after this, Slim."

"Jake, I swear to you I never—"

"Go wan! Get off of there!"

AFTERWARDS MORTON WISHED to go downstairs for further conversation with his friend Martin, so Sergeant Beddicker showed McGarvey around—showed him the radio room in the dome, where small brass counters on enormous maps marked the placement of every one of the 400-odd patrol cars, the switchboard room, the glassed-in teletype room; showed him the offices and museums of the narcotic and bomb squads, the identification bureau where fingerprint cards were contained in cases stretching to the ceiling, and where thousands of likenesses of male and female criminals were flat in the shallow steel drawers of filing cabinets; the ballistics bureau, where Sergeant Butts peered down a double microscope examining a chunk of lead.

Young McGarvey was fascinated, but he became, after a time, nervous as well. When Morton had been with him it was different. Alone with the saturnine Beddicker, he was troubled, self-conscious. He had never before thought of himself as a Southerner; but now, among those crisp, chilled, fast-talking New Yorkers, he became acutely aware of his speech, of his clothes, of his very movements, shambling like those of a bear. He believed that these precise and arrogant policemen were snickering at him behind his back.

"How 'bout lunch?" asked Beddicker.

"I better see what Mort's doing first."

But Morton already had gone out with Martin, leaving word that he would return at about two-thirty. So McGarvey, uneasy though he was, went with Sergeant Beddicker.

Afterward, in the corridor which led to the commissioner's office Beddicker told seven or eight fellow cops the story.

"Funniest damn thing you ever saw! Here the guy's been you-alling all over the plant, and asking more dumb questions than a woman, and whenever anything came up he'd always say that this Mort, who's his sidekick, would know about that. Sure. This guy Mort, whoever he is, must be the smartest guy in the world!

"But anyway, what I was going to tell you, I take him out to the Olympic, and we run into Wasserman and Flynn and Ray Hubbard, and Ray catches the 'you-all' stuff and the 'I reckon' stuff, and I get Ray's eye and hand him a wink, and to the other boys, too, and then I start peddling a line of crap about the guys around us. There's the usual bunch. Mostly cops, but a few cab drivers and some truck drivers and so-forth.

"Well, I tell this guy that this is a hangout for all kinds of dangerous crooks and gangsters, and I start pointing out guys to him and telling him they're famous racketeers. Say, it was a riot! He ate it up like nobody's business. But the funniest part came when Ray Hubbard, who gets the idea right away, points to a little flea-bitten guy alone over in a corner there, and tells this Southern flatfoot that it's Scoots Belinsky, the smartest racket backer in the city. Scoots Belinsky! Ray thinks it up just like that! What a card that boy is! He says this Belinsky is a millionaire a good many times over, but he always patronizes the Olympic when he's in this neighborhood because that's where he first got his start as a dishwasher. He says this Belinsky was really the brains behind Dutch Schultz and Waxey Gordon and all the rest of them. And this kid wants to know why we don't pick him up then, if we know so much about him. And you know what he tells us?" Beddicker, choking with laughter, leaned against a wall. "He tells us that if a guy like that was in Florida, this guy Morton would nail him in no time at all! And then he says—"

McGarvey had swung into sight at the end of the corridor and was approaching with long strides. McGarvey
stood six feet three, and weighed almost two hundred and
fifty pounds, and each of his fists was like a Westphalian
ham, only not so soft. Just now his face was red as building
bricks, and his eyes were not reassuring.

McGarvey, after lunch, had expressed a desire to look at
the headquarters building from the outside, and it was this
which had given Beddicker his chance to duck inside and
tell the boys the funny, funny story. Well, it so happened
that around behind the building, opposite the clutter of
clothing shops and newspapermen's cubbyholes, McGarvey had chanced upon the man Beddicker had pointed
out to him as Scoots Belinsky. This person's right name
was Magradian, or something like that, and he was an
Armenian who for business purposes posed as a Turk. His
humble luncheon finished, he had donned again his phony,
moth-eaten, once-crimson fez, and had returned to his
usual work of pushing a small wagon piled with a sticky
white or pinkish substance which a sign proclaimed to be
REAL TURKISH HALVAH 5 CENTS.

McGarvey thereupon had gone back into headquarters,
his face red with fury.

Beddicker's gaunt face tightened a little, but he managed
to produce a grin. He asked, with strained affability,
whether McGarvey had got a good look around outside.

"Sure, I saw a lot! Like I see a lot in here!" McGarvey
stepped close to Beddicker. "A lot of wisecrackers who'd be
better off if they went out and took on something tough for
a change and stopped shipping torpedos down to Florida
to shoot up places with guns from here!"

"What—what are you talking about anyway?"

But the laughter all around, the laughter that puffed out lips and cheeks and emerged in choppy snorts through distended nostrils, was audible now. The boys just couldn't keep it in.

"What I'm talking about is that if you overgrown lice knew anything about your business you'd be out busting up this gun ring instead of horsing around here like a lot of—"

"Maybe," Beddicker cut in, "if they made your friend Mort commissioner he could show them how they—"

McGarvey hit him on the left cheekbone. It sounded like *"Woo-oomp!"* Beddicker went backward two swift steps, hit the shoulder of one of his pals, whirled completely around and fell.

Turning, McGarvey had a fleet glimpse of somebody coming toward him with raised hands. The fellow, a uniformed cop, only intended to grab McGarvey's arms, but McGarvey didn't stop to figure this out. McGarvey hit him.

Whereupon the rest of the boys, being human, piled in.

They say of him in Miami, where they idolize him, that Wentworth L. Morton has a genius for appearing at the right moment. Well, he did it that afternoon in New York headquarters, and with him was Deputy Commissioner Martin, who shouted: "Here! What *is* this?"

Panting, sweating, they backed away like schoolboys surprised. One of the men muttered that it was nothing but a friendly roughhouse, no harm intended. The others nodded, except Beddicker, who was on his knees, and McGarvey.

"Well, it certainly is a fine idea, right outside the

commissioner's office practically. Now clear out of here! Can't Beddicker get up? Get him up and take him away from here."

"Sure, get him up," said McGarvey. "I want to knock him down again."

Morton grabbed his partner, whirled him around. "Listen, ape! You get downstairs and wait for me at that information booth. We're going on the Florida Special this afternoon, instead of going tonight. I guess I can't trust you out of my sight in this town!"

When the battlers had departed, Morton apologized to Martin, and Martin apologized back to Morton, and they shook hands.

"This Cro-Magnon man," Morton explained, "is a good kid, but he gets excited easy. He's old man McGarvey's son. You remember old Garv? Well, this kid's just like him— only worse, if anything. Well, g'by, commissioner. Look me up if you get down to the Beach next winter."

"I'll do that. Sorry about the fuss."

"Forget it!"

4

McGARVEY PICKS UP A TRAIL

THEY CHECKED OUT of their hotel, they got their prisoner, they started uptown for Penn Station. *That* sight, at least, McGarvey was to see! He sat in a corner of the cab, glowering. Handcuffed to his left wrist was Maurice "Whitey" Wilson, who was a stringy little man, a whimperer, a crawler, with sickly green eyes and colorless thin hair and a mouth that twitched. Once Whitey had been a celebrated automobile driver, a man of steel-cold nerve. But he was inherently crooked, and the result was that he was ruled off every track in the country. He had turned quite naturally to crime. More recently he had taken to heroin.

"If you guys would just believe me when I tell you—" he whined.

"Sure," cut in Morton. "You whisper to somebody somewhere that you want artillery, and right away it rains guns. But you never know who the guy was you whispered to. You said already."

"That's all I know! Honest! This guy I tell, he's not the one knows about it. He just passes on the word, and after a while—"

"And after a while you walk into a hotel room or an

32

apartment, in whatever place it is you're going to pull the job, and there's a flock of guns waiting for you. Sure. They come from nowhere, I suppose?"

"That's all I know! Absolutely! Why, if I knew—"

"Oh, shut up," said Morton.

McGarvey was staring moodily out of the cab window. When they were halted by traffic, somewhere in Seventh Avenue, he cried suddenly: "There's that guy Walkely, over in that bar! They must have let him go!"

"Well, what could they have held him on?"

"If those guys would only—"

"Oh, for Gawd's sake! Do I have to listen to all that again?"

The concourse of Penn Station, viewed from any angle, is a mighty impressive place. McGarvey was all eyes. He strode ahead, paying no attention to the cringing figure fastened to his wrist, who was like a child trying to keep up to an impatient father.

They had come out of the taxicab ramp, and were passing the base of the grand stairway leading to Thirty-first Street. Morton, who had paid the cab driver, was a little behind. He was fumbling in his pockets for the tickets.

There were four shots, blurred almost into one, and they made a terrific noise even in that great place. Three times Whitey Wilson was buffeted by the shock of lead, and each time his body jerked at the handcuffs. Then he collapsed.

His collapse spun McGarvey around. He got his pistol out, but for an instant he wasn't set to shoot. Morton was down, on his side, but he, too, had a pistol in his right fist, and though he was otherwise motionless his eyes moved back and forth. Without looking at his partner he shouted:

"Not here, Garv! You'll kill somebody!"

A third pistol was skimming across the smooth shiny floor. A big black thing, it slid twenty yards before it struck a woman on the foot. She screamed, and promptly fainted. The pistol, only slightly deflected, skidded on across the concourse.

It was incredible, and yet it had happened. It had happened all at once. McGarvey roared "Stop!" and fired twice toward the ceiling. The cast-off gun, which had miraculously missed other persons, at last came to a stop underneath the air transport exhibit. A dozen women screamed, and three fainted. People ran. People fell flat. One fellow, who had been half way down the steps from Thirty-first Street, stiffened in fright, toppled like a dummy, and bumped down step after step, winding up with a broken shoulder blade. But most of the people in the station stood stock-still, paralyzed with fear; not thinking, not really seeing anything.

IT HAD HAPPENED. There was McGarvey, fuming, manacled to a bloody corpse; and there was Morton, white as a sheet, vainly calling commands that nobody should quit the immediate vicinity.

McGarvey was bellowing with rage, trying to jerk himself free, trying to get to the side of Morton.

"Are you hurt?"

"Do you think I'm lying here because it's so nice and soft? Here," he threw McGarvey the handcuffs key, "get busy!"

The one person who might have told the story was dead. Maurice "Whitey" Wilson lay with bulging eyes, his mouth open as though to scream. He had seen death coming, and had recognized the dealer of death. Too late.

Morton poopoohed his wound all the way to the hospital.

"Hell, it's only through a muscle of the leg! I'll be out in two days. Little rest will do me good. Make me less crabby maybe."

No detective was amazed when the pistol proved to be a Colt .45 automatic recently stolen from an armory in Brooklyn.

"The dear old army," Morton sighed.

McGarvey spluttered: "If these cops up here knew their business! Instead of horsing around with a lot of—if they only knew that—"

"Oh, it's as much Washington's responsibility as it is theirs. That's one reason they're both so anxious to break up the ring—both the cops and the Department of Justice boys. Whenever one manages to horn in on the publicity for a piece of good work the others pulled, they both give out statements about how they 'cooperated.' Yeah! Sure!" Mort said.

"I don't think either of them know what they're doing!"

Morton, who had just been put to bed, and around whom nurses were fussing, looked sharply at his partner.

"Listen, Tarzan," he said. "I don't want you busting in on something you don't know anything about and getting in a lot of trouble just because I'm not there to watch you. Keep out of this thing, understand! You got a break now. You got a couple of days you didn't expect. Well, use 'em. Go out and see Grant's Tomb and the Empire State Building and all those art museums you were talking about, and for cripe's sake keep that mug of yours out of fights!"

The doctor shooed McGarvey away. The patient must rest, the doctor said. No visitors until nine o'clock the next morning.

Morton, wise old Morton, with troubled eyes, watched the giant go.

"You remember what I told you now!"

"Yeah... sure," said McGarvey.

And McGarvey, as a matter of fact, did do a little sight-seeing, once he was able to escape from reporters. But his heart wasn't in the thing. Then suddenly, when it was still early evening, he decided to go looking for Slim Walkely.

It wasn't easy for him to find the bar in Seventh Avenue, where from a taxi he had seen Walkely, but when he did find the place he was sure of it.

It was not an ex-speakeasy soaked with blowsy memories, but one of these still-new, post-repeal establishments whose ambitious proprietors are pitifully affable and good-fellowy. More than a year old, it still looked brand new, and it was crowded.

McGARVEY SAT THERE for three hours. He was uncomfortable. In the first place, he was worried about Morton. Then, he retained much of the feeling of embarrassment he had suffered in Centre Street; he continued to be conscious of the fact that he was a hick, a hayseed, a man with a funny accent. Further, he was not a drinker—never touched a drop, and disapproved of drinking as he did of smoking and gambling—and whenever he was obliged to remain long in the presence of exposed liquor the odor usually made him sick.

He got a table to himself, in a corner, from where he could watch the bar, and he ordered a highball and a ham-on-rye. The sandwich he ate. The highball he dumped, little by little, into a cuspidor.

Perhaps, at that, he had picked a good place from which to see New York; though he didn't think so. The city banged and thundered around him, and screeched and bawled and rattled, while he sat there being miserable. He saw drunks and barflies and chiselers—but they looked the same as the chiselers, barflies and drunks he had seen so often in his native Miami. He was discouraged. Probably Slim Walkely didn't come into this place regularly, after all. And, besides, what should McGarvey do if Slim *did* come?

Now he had a headache. He became thirsty because of the ham, and, dumping the rest of his highball into the spittoon, he ordered a straight rye with a water chaser; then he drank the chaser and prepared to send the rye after the highball. The bar had an expensive new ventilating system, but it wasn't working, and cigarette smoke made McGarvey cough and blink. Possibly he looked the part he was trying to play; possibly with his bloodshot eyes, his strained mouth, and vacant stare, he seemed a solitary drunkard.

Anyway, he needed air. If he didn't get out of this dive pretty soon he'd be sick all over the floor.

He had paid the waiter and was rising to his feet, a trifle groggy, when Slim Walkely came in.

Walkely didn't see McGarvey, who stepped quickly into a telephone booth. The fur-cutter greeted the bartender boisterously, but his joviality seemed a bit frayed, and there was worriment in his eyes as he looked around the café. He saw a man at a far distant table, nodded, went there. They whispered. Presently the man got up, turning, and made for a booth directly next to the booth in which McGarvey stood. McGarvey heard him dial a number, ask for John— and then the door was closed.

McGarvey leaned close to the thin partition, but the man's voice was low, his words a mere mumble.

But unexpectedly one name came clear. Evidently the party at the other end wished to be sure of this name, which wasn't familiar to him, and the man in the booth next to McGarvey raised his voice to pronounce it slowly and carefully, twice. "Boca Raton— That's it, Boca Raton." Then he spelled it, to make sure: "B-o-c-a R-a-t-o-n."

Why, that was the name of a town in Florida! A town where McGarvey himself had a cousin he was always meaning to visit, but never did!

What was the connection? Boca Raton was a small place, and, so far as McGarvey knew, there had been no gangster activity there, no recent crimes of violence. A quiet little place. What could it have to do with a man who had just been whispering with Slim Walkely?

McGarvey could hear no more of the conversation, though he tried. Indeed, he tried so hard that he almost missed seeing Slim Walkely leave.

Well, McGarvey didn't know who this man in the next booth was, and didn't know whether he had anything to do with the army gun ring, but Walkely, he felt sure, was involved. He had no proof of this. But McGarvey's wasn't a logical mind. He was an emotional cuss, a creature of his impulses. So he followed Walkely.

5

DEATH STRIKES AGAIN

THE FUR CUTTER, whose police record showed that he actually had engaged in that occupation at one time, drifted west to Eighth Avenue, turned south. It was late May, but the night was chilly, and McGarvey, his blood thinned by a lifetime in southern Florida, shivered and jammed his hands deeper into his pockets.

Down Eighth Avenue several blocks, then right toward the river. Walkely went slowly, seemingly without any fixed destination, and never looked back. He turned down Ninth Avenue, shadow-packed under the silent El. He turned left, went back to Eighth Avenue, then turned left again, and yet again at the next block. McGarvey began to be troubled. Walkely made still another left turn, sauntering back into Ninth Avenue.

McGarvey scudded around the corner—and saw Walkely watching him from a doorway.

There was nobody else in sight. Walkely was crouched back, one hand on the doorknob, the other, his right, in his coat pocket. His eyes were open wide, and there was fear in them when first he stared at McGarvey. Fear—and then, immediately afterward, relief. Walkely relaxed. He grinned a little.

McGarvey, to save face, walked on. He pretended that he was not in the least interested in this man in the doorway. But his face, for all the chill of the night, burned red with humiliation.

He heard a low, juicy chuckle behind him, and then the sound of a door closed gently. He turned. Slim Walkely had disappeared.

McGarvey paused, irresolute. He had not at any time really known what he was going to do if and when he did get his hands on Slim Walkely in some quiet place. Vaguely he supposed that he'd paste Walkely's jaw for him a few times and get the truth out of the man. But this was as far as he had planned. And now Walkely had stepped away from him.

Walkely had known that he was being followed, and had contrived to get a look at the man following him. He had been horribly frightened, then relieved. McGarvey was not what he'd expected.

Finally he had been amused at the awkwardness of the big fellow. It was the memory of this amusement which infuriated McGarvey.

McGarvey went back to the door. It led into an ancient wooden structure, absurdly small, only three stories high and about ready to fall apart. The ground floor was an unoccupied store, smudgy and dark. The second floor, too, seemed to be deserted. Its windows were blank and bare, and astoundingly dirty. But as McGarvey watched, light appeared in the third story windows, and he saw shades there and even some sleazy curtains.

Should he go in? He wished Morton was with him, to tell him. He had no authority in this city, either as a detective or a deputy sheriff. What would he do upstairs? What *could* he do, confronting Walkely?

"What the hell do you think you're doing around here?"

McGarvey turned. This patrolman was big, and he was Irish, and he didn't like McGarvey's looks any more than McGarvey liked his. He was the kind of man who thinks he's tough just because he happens to be disagreeable.

"Looking for somebody? What's the matter—can't you talk?"

Possibly it was the uniform; possibly it was a remembrance of Morton's warning to keep out of trouble; possibly it was the realization that a fight, an arrest, would make Morton furious and bring delight to Beddicker and those other smart-alecs in Centre Street. Whatever it was, for once in his life McGarvey held his temper.

"Looking for a party named Campbell," he said meekly, for him. "Between Twenty-ninth and Thirtieth."

The patrolman waved his stick disgustedly. "Up that way. What's the matter with you? Can't you read signs?"

McGARVEY WENT UPTOWN a few blocks and then over to Eighth Avenue, where he had a cup of coffee in an all-light lunchroom. Then he went back to the place where he'd last seen Slim Walkely.

About twenty minutes had elapsed. The patrolman wasn't in sight. McGarvey, without any hesitation this time, went to the door, tried it, found that it was not locked, and entered.

The place was dark as pitch, and McGarvey, not being a smoker, had no matches. Feeling for the stairs, he tried to move quietly, but he knew he was making a lot of noise. Even if he hadn't been so sore at the cop on the beat, at

Slim Walkely for his sneer, at the boys in headquarters, at this whole damned city of New York, he would not have been able to go up those stairs in silence. They squealed and squeaked and shrilled and shrieked: they did every-thing but whistle.

A grayish light came ungraciously through the dirt of one small window on the second floor, in the rear. It helped a little. But when McGarvey turned his back to it and started feeling along the hand rail for the second flight of steps he was again in darkness. The bannister was coated with dust, which tickled his hand.

The bannister curved, and McGarvey turned with it. His feet found the stairs, and he started up, one step, two steps—

Then there was light, but it was a terrific stuttering light, sharp and very hot, and through it a long streamer of crim-son rolled languorously, coiled, uncoiled, burst. McGarvey fought back as best he could. Even in that horrible instant he realized that somebody had been waiting for him on the stairs—somebody who had seen him dimly as he came groping along the hall silhouetted against the pasty gray light from the window. And the somebody had a heavy weapon.

McGarvey got his left arm up, but another blow crushed all feeling from it. He stumbled backward, reaching for his gun. Still another blow hit his right elbow. Several must have missed him. The terrible white light was gone, and with it the red streamers, and to McGarvey the world had become one great roaring sound. He was aware that somebody was pushing past him. He reached out with both arms.

Then he was sitting down.

He heard somebody run down the stairs, open and close the street door.

It was perhaps a half minute later that he was able to get to his feet. Going downstairs was very difficult. He kept lurching against the bannister or thumping the wall with his shoulder. Near the bottom his feet seemed to go up in the air, and he pitched down the last four or five steps, sprawling on hands and knees upon a dusty, splintery floor.

He got up again, cursing Slim Walkely. He staggered for the door, fumbled for it, found it, opened it.

His head was clearing now. He closed the door again, leaned against it from the inside, and tried to dope things out.

He had seen that the block outside was deserted except for one person, the last person McGarvey wished to have see him come out of this house, the truculent cop on the beat, who leaned against the El pillar and twirled his stick.

So McGarvey went, instead, upstairs.

This time he went with one arm held above his head. It wasn't likely that he would meet anyone else, but he wasn't taking any chances.

A front door on the third floor was ajar and light came from it. McGarvey drew and cocked his gun, kicked open the door, jumped aside.

"Come out and take it," he called.

There was no sound from the room. McGarvey, crouching very low, and with his gun in front of him, peered around the edge. He saw a pair of feet. He grunted and went in.

It hadn't been Slim Walkely who clouted him. Slim

wasn't going to clout anybody again, with anything. He was stretched out flat on his face, just inside the doorway, and the back of his head was anything but pretty.

McGARVEY STEPPED OVER him, swiftly searched the room, being careful to keep away from the windows. There was nothing—or almost nothing. Some cracked furniture. Two hand bags, both open, only half unpacked. A few toilet articles.

Then McGarvey turned back to the corpse.

The well-known blunt instrument had been used, and with spirit. A blackjack maybe, more likely a gas pipe or something like that. The weapon was not in the apartment. There was nothing about Walkely's position to indicate that he had made any resistance. His arms were spread wide; his hands, clawed, were empty. His pockets had been turned out.

McGarvey's guess was that he had never known what hit him. He had been struck from behind as he stepped into the apartment. The first blow probably knocked him flat; possibly it killed him; but the murderer had hit him again and again, to be sure of the job.

There was no telephone in the apartment, or McGarvey would have reported the murder promptly. He was, after all, a cop.

He found matches in Walkely's pocket, and went down to the second floor. There were three doors, but each of them was locked, and each lock was coated with rust. With what matches remained, McGarvey examined the place where the murderer, escaping, had waited for him. There were footprints in the dusty stairs, but they were too scuffled to be of any assistance to a detective like this one. But he did find one interesting thing. It was a button, a gray bone button. There wasn't any dust on it. Apparently it had been torn from a coat. A slim shred of brownish material clung to it. McGarvey pocketed this, and went out.

He looked up and down. It seemed to him incredible that any street in New York City, even at midnight, could be utterly deserted. He sought a lighted window, a telephone.

A hand fell on his shoulder.

"So yuh were looking for a man named Campbell, huh?"

This time McGarvey did not even try to hold himself in. The whirling motion the cop himself had started, McGarvey finished as a right-hander from down near his knee. He grunted with delight as his knuckles whammed against that square Irish chin.

One was enough. One like that. The patrolman, almost as big a man as McGarvey himself, stumbled against the store window, bumped it. Then his legs became like rubber bands. He pitched forward.

Now it's a serious offense, even in New York, to knock a policeman down. McGarvey, for the first time, got a little panicky. So many explanations would be needed! So much pull! And meanwhile the murderer of Slim Walkely—

Say, how would McGarvey be able to prove that he himself hadn't killed Walkely? Certainly this patrolman, when he returned from slumberland—and already he was stirring—would not be a pleasant witness.

So, what with one thing and another, McGarvey decided to run.

He ran general north and west, and very soon he was

lost. Near some large docks, however, he found scores of taxicabs. It seems there was a midnight sailing.

"Take me to Penn Station," said McGarvey.

In Penn Station he would at least know where he was. And it was a good place to have gone if they tried to trace his movements. For by this time he was beginning to understand how criminals hot from their crime must feel. He wondered whether men he had pursued felt this way.

The terminal was quiet now, McGarvey would have liked to look around, but he didn't have time.

Out on the sidewalk again he paused. He wished to hell he had Morton with him! Morton would have seen a lot of things he was probably missing. For a mild moment he thought of going to the hospital. Then he remembered how vehement the doctor had been about the need for sleep, and he knew he wouldn't even be allowed to see his partner.

Up the avenue, opposite the station, were the lights of the Hotel Pennsylvania. Hotels have all sorts of telephone books. McGarvey went to the Pennsylvania.

Manhattan, Bronx, Queens, Richmond, Brooklyn, Nassau, Suffolk, Westchester, Hudson, Essex—no result. But when he got to work on the Bergen County book he found one at last.

It was in New Jersey. The book didn't say whether it was a club, or a restaurant, or a hotel, or what, but simply: "Boca Raton, Cliff Rd." That must be the place.

McGarvey went to the bell captain.

"Say, whereabouts could I get one of these drive-your-self cars?"

6

WITHIN A DESERTED HOUSE

TAKING EVERYTHING INTO consideration, McGarvey was seeing a lot of sights in New York at that. Police headquarters, Flower Hospital, Penn Station, and now the George Washington Bridge.

Unfortunately the river wasn't looking its best that night. In fact, most of the time he couldn't see the water at all; fog, lolling up from the bay, blotted it out. Through that fog McGarvey could hear the solemn, spaced boo-oops of river craft sliding past below, and the clang of dock bells.

Was it the biggest bridge in the world? McGarvey wasn't certain, at first. Couldn't remember. But before he got to the New Jersey end he was sure that it was.

A cop stopped chewing and said scornfully: "The Boca Raton? The roadhouse? Yeah. It's up the line a little ways. Closed now though."

"Already? It's not much after twelve."

The cop looked pityingly at him.

"Been closed four months now," he said, and walked away.

Disconcerting information; but McGarvey had come all the way over that bridge, and he'd paid for this erratic old automobile and he didn't know where else to go anyway. So he continued.

The Boca Raton once had been a private mansion, and it was very large, very grand, and badly in need of repair. It not only stood in Cliff Road, alone; it practically *was* that thoroughfare. Damp, dismal, it showed no light. Its windows, downstairs, were covered by boards; upstairs they gleamed wan and unblinking, great eyes glazed with evil. A deep veranda, from the pillars of which dirty gray paint was peeling, went around three sides. In front, facing Cliff Road, which was not much more than a private drive, hung a sign which said "Boca Raton," and which once had been loud with colored electric bulbs but now hung listless, dark, a ghost of departed gayety. A grim silence held reign over it all.

McGarvey did not drive into Cliff Road. He parked the Buick some distance away, and walked. For several minutes, hidden in a clump of evergreen, he surveyed this disconsolate pile. It looked as though it had not been occupied for four years, rather than four months.

He started for it. Somebody grabbed his elbow.

"Just a minute! Where do you think you're going?"

Not a friendly voice at all. Nor was the grip friendly. McGarvey's right hand had been over his gun, and now instinctively he lifted it.

"Don't do that!"

And in view of what he felt against his belly, McGarvey decided to obey this command.

"Take your hand out, slowly, and be sure it's empty!"

McGarvey did this. He was wishing he could see the

man's face under the brim of the felt. He bent his knees a little, squinting.

"Oh," he murmured. "The guy that was talking to Slim Walkely!"

"What do you know about Slim Walkely?"

McGarvey said: "Guess."

For a moment they stared at one another, the man still pressing the gun into McGarvey's belly, and McGarvey with his hands shoulder high. Then a grin spread very slowly over the giant's face.

It was a confident, knowing grin. It said: "So you think I'm here alone, do you?" And it had its effect upon the gunman, who stepped back. He held the gun firm, but not close to his hip.

McGarvey's eyes flicked right for an instant. The man looked in that direction. And McGarvey jumped him.

The gun went up, the man holding it went over backward, and McGarvey, all two hundred and fifty pounds of him, landed full and fair upon the man. The thud seemed violent enough to start an avalanche on the near-by Palisades. Afterward, the man didn't move. The breath had been knocked out of him, and his head had thumped the hard ground.

McGARVEY GOT UP carefully, and carefully he disengaged the forefinger of his left hand, upon which the revolver's hammer had fallen. That was why the revolver hadn't gone off.

McGarvey uncocked the gun, put it into one of his own pockets, and looked around, listening.

There was nobody in sight. There was nothing to indicate that this little tussle had been witnessed. A couple of hundred yards away two automobiles whirred along the highway. The mournful, monotonous sound of foghorns ascended from the river.

Now what? He certainly wished Mort was here.

The man was beginning to moan. His eyelids twitched, his mouth twitched. Hastily McGarvey took off necktie and belt, ripped the shirt to strips. It wasn't a very good job of binding and gagging he made, but it was the best he could do under the circumstances. He hauled the man, conscious now and glaring, back into the evergreen. He went to the house.

Front and back doors were locked. The boards over the downstairs windows were such that not even a man of McGarvey's strength could easily rip them off—certainly not without making a lot of noise. The cellar windows were backed by thick steel bars.

"Must be some way to get in," he muttered.

It was chilly, and he shivered. A wisp of fog wandered past him. He glanced back toward the place where he had left his prisoner, and saw that the evergreen was trembling. The man must be wriggling around, trying to escape. McGarvey shrugged.

He went up on the veranda, grasped a pillar, stepped upon the rail. He began to shinny.

The wood was rotten, and became crumby in his hands with a little pressure. But the edge of the roof itself was good and firm, and soon McGarvey had pulled his bulk over that. The roof was a tin one, but new, and didn't clack under his feet.

All the windows were locked, but he found one which

was so flimsy that a little pushing clicked it open. He went in.

There seemed to be no furniture at all upstairs. The place was damp, clammy.

On the first floor he found a deserted barroom, some empty bottles, stacked-up tables and chairs. The dance floor was bleak and bare. At one end was a platform, and on this remained the shields which once had marked individual jazz players; each shield was frosted like an expensive old-fashioned Christmas card, and each bore the gilt words "Bertie's Boys."

There was not a tingle of merriment left in the air. It seemed as though it must have been years and years since Bertie's Boys had made their music in this place.

The cellar contained a cold furnace, some lumber, some broken chairs, and uncountable beer and liquor cases, all empty.

McGarvey started for the steps.

Then he smelled cigarette smoke.

A non-smoker himself, he was notably sensitive to the smell of tobacco. Now he paused, sniffing the air. Yes, there could be no doubt about it. And it was somewhere near at hand.

When he stopped to think of it, the cellar *did* appear to be small for such a mansion. He turned back from the steps and with outstretched arms and feeling fingers began to search the place more carefully.

Presently he found a steel door. The handle turned, and he pushed it open. It didn't make a sound.

Until this time he had been going entirely by feel, but now he had a light for guidance. It came from a rectangular opening, about chin-high, in another steel door, on the right. The opening was like an old speakeasy peek-hole, only smaller.

Opposite was another door, with a similar opening, but this one was dark.

McGARVEY BEGAN TO understand. A man caught between these two doors, assuming that there were guards behind each of them, would be in a very bad position indeed. He wouldn't have a chance in the world of getting out alive, if it so happened that those guards didn't want him to.

McGarvey went to the lighted opening, peered in.

He could see only a small portion of the room beyond—what appeared to be the center of the room. A single electric bulb hung from the ceiling. Under that was a table, and seated at the table was a man smoking a cigarette and reading the *Racing Form.*

He was a short man, but powerfully built, a truncated Samson, with the arms and shoulders of an orang-outang. His face was pimply, and he needed a shave. He squinted or frowned as he read, as if the light was bad, though it wasn't.

On the table—it was a big table—was a sawed-off shotgun, two Thompson sub-machine guns, two revolvers, four automatic pistols, a French-type telephone looking ludicrously out of place, several boxes of cartridges, a box of shotgun shells, and three extra drums for the Thompsons.

Cautiously McGarvey tried the door. It was locked. He stepped back. He examined this small, steel-lined anteroom even more closely, and made doubly certain that there was no guard behind the opposite door. Then deliberately he rattled the knob of the door by which he had entered the anteroom.

He flattened himself against the door under the lighted rectangle. His gun was out, and he was holding his breath.

A switch clicked, and there was bright light in the anteroom. He heard the man pick up at least one of the weapons from the table, heard him approach the door. Then, when he figured that the man would be just about to put his eye to the rectangle, he rose, showing his gun muzzle in that space.

"Move and you get it!"

There was a startled grunt. McGarvey, staring along his pistol barrel, could see that he had estimated well. The orang-outang's face was within two inches of the muzzle.

"Don't step back! Don't lift your hands!"

He was taking, of course, the terrible chance that the man was not alone. He had only been able to see part of the room.

"Drop whatever you're holding!"

Something clattered to the floor inside.

"What's in the other hand too. Drop it!"

The man shook his head.

McGarvey whispered: "Would you like a skullful, guy?"

"Ain't got anything in the other hand. Gawd's honest truth, boss!"

"All right. Raise both hands slow then, but be sure your fingers are spread wide! Hold 'em away from your body."

The hands came up empty.

"All right. Now, moving like you were handling a bottle of nitroglycerine, I want you to unlock this door."

There would have to be an instant, as the door was

being swung open, in which McGarvey's gun was not covering the orang-outang. McGarvey knew this, and the orang-outang knew it. But McGarvey was a thought ahead of the orang-outang. The instant he heard the click of the lock he took his gun away from the rectangle and threw himself against the door.

The guard hadn't expected that. When the gun muzzle disappeared he had stooped, meaning to recover the gun he'd dropped. The door hit him, shoving him back toward the table.

McGarvey, in the open doorway now, yelled: *"Don't do it!"*

But the orang-outang tried. He lunged for the table. He was fast for a man of that build. Actually he had scooped up one of the automatics when the giant from Florida started firing.

McGarvey fired three shots. Then he raised the barrel of his gun. The sharp smell of powder stung his eyes. He shook his head.

"Well, I told you not to try that."

But there wasn't any answer. There couldn't be any answer. The distance hadn't been great, the light was good, and McGarvey was no slouch with a pistol. If he'd thought he could afford to, he would have winged the man in a shoulder or arm. As it was, he had shot to kill. Which was just what he did.

7

WHOLESALE DEATH

THE ROOM WAS not large. There were four doors leading from it, in addition to the door through which McGarvey had come. He tried each of these in turn. He took no chances, but kept his gun raised and cocked, and stood to one side before throwing open each door.

The doors led to closets. Big closets. And each closet was filled to the ceiling. There were seven dozen cases of Springfields and two cases of old Ross rifles. There was a case of automatic rifles. There were sixteen sub-machine guns. One closet, the biggest, contained only pistols, hundreds of them, mostly Colt .45 automatics, the army's 1911 model; but there were also thick batches of the 1917 model Smith and Wesson .45 revolvers, hanging from the ceiling with wires passed through their butt swivels. Another closet held, on shelves, Very pistols and other flares, gas masks, hand grenades, bullet-proof vests, tear gas bombs, incendiary bombs. In still another were heaped thousands of cartridge boxes, all of them full.

"Boy, oh boy! This thing was big business!" McGarvey breathed.

He examined again what was left of the orang-outang. No, this fellow had not been the head of the gun ring, the brains, the armorer to the underworld. This fellow had been nothing but a hired guard, a thug.

The possibility that he might not be alone haunted McGarvey, made him nervous. It didn't seem possible that such a valuable and incriminating stock of hardware would be left, even in this remote place, without better protection.

When the telephone rang he shied from it like a frightened girl. It seemed so real, so personal, here in this subterranean vault which McGarvey shared with a dead man. It rang and rang.

At last he raised the instrument. Gruffly: "Yeah?"

The voice was harsh, low: "You took long enough! Get over here right away! I need you!"

"But—"

"Never mind the buts. Get over here, both of you! There's going to be trouble and I need you here!"

Then the line went dead.

McGarvey said, as he held the connection down for a moment: "Yeah, there's going to be trouble all right. But whereabouts?" He took his finger away.

The operator wouldn't tell him where the call had come from. He tried asking her crisply, matter-of-factly; then he tried coaxing; then bullying. All she gave him was the chief operator.

McGarvey told the chief operator that he was a policeman and that this was important. She asked him if he were a Fort Lee policeman, and he said no, that he was from New York. It would mean too much explanation to say Miami. He said she could call up Spring 7-3100 and ask about him, if she didn't believe him—though he hoped she wouldn't do this, for he wasn't acquainted with any officer who'd be on duty in Centre Street at this hour. He cajoled, wheedled, coaxed, begged until, finally, probably more to get rid of him than for any other reason, she gave him the number and the address.

The call had come from the Hotel Besser in Central Park West, New York City. Whereabouts in the Besser? They didn't know that. Their listing simply gave it as the Hotel Besser. Presumably a switchboard there.

McGarvey hung up.

This was much too big a job for one man, as even he realized. He knew his duty. He ought to call the New York police and have them send somebody to the Besser, and then call the local police and report the killing of the orang-outang. He was about to do this when he heard somebody walking across the first floor, overhead.

THE SECOND INSIDE guard? The party at the Hotel Besser had said "both of you." This lighted room, McGarvey thought, would not be a good place to wait. He picked up the chair the orang-outang had been sitting on a short while before, and with this he went out to the cellar proper, being careful to close the doors behind him.

He didn't want any more shooting. He wanted silence now.

He was obliged again to go by feel. The man upstairs, however, seemed to be in the same predicament; he moved heavily, but slowly.

McGarvey found the steps, and waited. He heard the visitor open the door from the kitchen, heard him start down.

A voice called suddenly: "They didn't have Fatimas, so I got you Camels."

McGarvey stood to one side, and got a better grip on the chair. This, McGarvey reflected, was going to be a dirty trick. But what the hell!

The man stumbled, cursed.

"I suppose the chief's right about no lights until we're inside," he called, "but it certainly is one lousy nuisance when you're—"

It was utterly dark, and McGarvey, in swinging the chair, had aimed at the voice. The man made a lot of noise falling the last two or three steps, and then he was still.

On hands and knees, McGarvey felt for and found him. He ran his hands over the man's face; mustache, a stubble. The face was thin and hard. It was that of a young man. He was breathing. McGarvey found some blood on the top of the head—not much—and a blackjack in one of the pockets.

"I guess you're good for a while," muttered McGarvey.

He left the way he'd come, shinnying down the same pillar and picking up lots of splinters in the process. He went directly to the clump of evergreen, meaning to ask his prisoner, who had looked well dressed and intelligent, something about this place.

There was no sign of the prisoner. An automobile drew to a stop at the other end of Cliff Road. Six men got out and started for the Boca Raton, spreading as they moved. Of the two he could see best, one carried a sawed-off shotgun, the other a machine gun.

"Maybe Mort was right," Mort's partner whispered to himself. "Maybe I better not get in any trouble."

And so, with what was for him a rare display of discretion, he crept by a circuitous route back to the highway and to his rented automobile.

THE NIGHT SWITCHBOARD operator at the Hotel Besser, which was a quiet, ultra-respectable sort of place, said he was sorry but they didn't give out any record of telephone calls. McGarvey flashed a badge. It happened to be a Dade County deputy sheriff's badge, but the switchboard operator didn't get a good enough look at it to read this. He was frightened. He told McGarvey, who believed him, that he had just come on duty ten minutes ago, at one o'clock. There hadn't been any calls since then. He didn't find a record of any since midnight. But the other operator, he admitted, was pretty careless about keeping his record, especially when it was getting late and he was tired.

"Maybe you better speak to the night manager?"

"No," said McGarvey.

He thought for awhile. Without Morton, he had been doing a lot of thinking this night. Much more than he was accustomed to. And the strain was telling on him. But presently his face brightened.

"The Besser... Say, isn't this the place where Mr. Hedbirn lives? Arthur Hedbirn, the art dealer?"

Yes, Mr. Hedbirn lived here. Had the penthouse. What's more, the operator believed that he was up there now, because as he'd come across the park, on his way to work, he noticed lights up there.

"Has he lived here long?"

"He was here when I got the job, three years ago."

"Then he'd probably know most of the other people here?"

"Sure. We haven't got so many, and they're all old-timers.

Place is only about a third full. Shall I ring Mr. Hedbirn for you?"

"No," said McGarvey. "I'll just go up unannounced and surprise him."

Well, Hedbirn was surprised. No doubt of it. He was flabbergasted. He looked like a man scarcely able to believe his eyes.

McGarvey grinned.

"Hell of a time to come calling on folks," he said, "but I understood you were still up, and I got something to ask you. But if you're busy—"

Arthur Hedbirn's face resumed its expression of benign amiability. He opened the door wide.

"Not at all! Come right in! This *is* an unexpected pleasure!"

Except that he wasn't wearing his coat, Hedbirn was as neatly dressed as ever. But his apartment was not what McGarvey had expected. The walls were covered with etchings and paintings, and the furniture was all antique and probably very valuable. But the place was in disorder. The rug was rumpled. Two bulging, closed suitcases rested on a chair; another was open on the floor.

"Not unpacked yet?"

"No, I—I've been busy. And so nervous about all that unfortunate business on the boat."

Hedbirn seemed still nervous. He moved from place to place, picking up things, putting them down.

"What I wanted to know," said McGarvey, "is about the people who live in this place and which one of them might have made a phone call about forty-five or fifty minutes ago. Funny thing to ask you, but I figure you might know what guest it is once I've told you why I want to know. Might be able to give me a hint, anyway."

"Why, yes. I suppose so. Glad to help, if I'm able to."

"This guy," said McGarvey, "would be a very tough guy, but smart and smooth. He'd have a low, quick way of talking, and maybe—"

What interrupted him was the sight of a brown tweed coat hung over one of the chairs. "Say, what—" he began.

"All right, McGarvey! Put your hands up!"

ARTHUR HEDBIRN LOOKED now like anything in the world but a benign, unworldly art dealer. His mouth was drawn back. His eyes were blue diamonds.

"Well, I'll be damned," whispered McGarvey.

"You'll be more than damned, you'll be drilled, if you don't put those hands up."

McGarvey put his hands up.

He said: "So you were the guy who—"

"Yes. I don't like men knowing who I am. I spent too much time and money building up this front to have it spoiled by punks I've hired for contact work."

"Meaning Wilson and Walkely."

"Yes, both of them. Whitey Wilson was all right, at first. He had swell connections. But I had to let him go when he began using dope. I took on Walkely. He was pretty good, too, for awhile. He had a record and was liable to be searched anywhere he went, but I could arrange that by taking the stuff myself. Naturally nobody ever thought to frisk me."

"Naturally. But why the bangbangs for Whitey?"

"All I wanted to do was see that he got put away for a long stretch where he wouldn't get heroin that might make him talk," Hedbirn explained. "When I heard he was going to be in on that job in Miami, which I had cased myself for boys who didn't even know me when they saw me, I decided that Rayford would be a good place. You don't have any parole system down there in Florida. So I tipped you off. I particularly asked for you because I'd heard you were quick with a gun. But you let Whitey get away. And then coming up on the boat you talked in such a way you had me scared that you could crack Whitey on the way back. I thought maybe you had something on him that I didn't know about, and that he might squeal. So I erased him myself. I took an awful chance, but I got away with it on my looks. People never think a murderer might have white hair and a fatherly smile. I slung the gun away and pretended to throw a faint. Then I slipped off in the excitement." He waved McGarvey back to a long couch, and made him sit on it. From time to time his eyes flicked nervously toward the door.

"Expecting somebody?" McGarvey asked.

"A couple of half-wits, yes." As he took the two guns from McGarvey his voice was flat, his hands quick and sure. He backed away. "But they're strong. Strong enough to carry you out of this place."

"Sure?"

"It won't be so hard. You'll be in a trunk."

"Oh." McGarvey swallowed, and his throat felt dusty. His head hurt. He was lying flat on the couch and Hedbirn, keen and watchful, was fully fifteen feet away. "You certainly don't like guys to know you, do you?"

"I've only been getting away with this gun peddling

because nobody has even suspected me, and I'm not going to have it spoiled now."

He got behind a little table. He cocked the two captured guns with his left hand and placed them side by side on this table, the muzzles turned toward his prisoner. Then he shifted his own gun to his left hand. All this time his eyes never left McGarvey.

"What was the matter with Slim Walkely?" McGarvey asked.

"I don't know for certain, but I think he was turning yellow. It must have been him who squealed to Wallie Faben's brother, here in New York, that I'd tipped you cops to the Miami job. Wallie Faben was the man you killed in that jewelry shop, and his brother liked him a lot. When I saw Walkely on the boat I suspected that there was something wrong. I'd changed my plans the last minute, and instead of going all the way back by train I'd got on the boat at Charleston. Walkely wasn't supposed to be on that boat too. He was working for me, but he wasn't supposed to recognize me in public. I didn't want to be seen talking to a man with a record. But when I saw him there I figured he might have agreed by long distance telephone to finger me for Wallie Faben's brother at the dock."

"Oh," said McGarvey.

HEDBIRN, WITH THE little table in front of him, and all the guns, looked curiously like a magician about to produce rabbits. He had taken a long thin silencer from a drawer in the table, and now, his eyes always on McGarvey, he was screwing this to the muzzle of his automatic.

"Then Walkely tossed a conference with a federal, tonight in Seventh Avenue. I was sure that he was making some deal with them. He might have been only telling about my gun drop. But then again, he might have been turning me in. So I went to his place and waited for him to come back. And then you had to come along. I didn't know it was you until just now, when I saw you staring at where that button used to be."

McGarvey's fury was subsiding, and he got a little sick at the realization of what a mess he'd made of this whole job. If only Morton was here! Fascinated, he watched Hedbirn screw the silencer on. He knew Hedbirn couldn't allow him to go away alive, under the circumstances.

8

MCGARVEY TAKES A BOW

AND THEN, ASTOUNDINGLY, incredibly, Morton was coming across the room! Wentworth L. Morton of Miami, Fla., pale, limping a little, but moving quickly, his gun in his hand. He had come from the bedroom, and now he was approaching Hedbirn from behind.

It flashed through McGarvey's mind that he was delirious. He was worn out, overheated by excitement, panicky perhaps in the near presence of death, and with a head which throbbed still from the pounding it had received at the hands of this man who was going to kill him. He was seeing things! He closed his eyes, squeezed them. And then opened them again—and still saw Morton.

"That act of trying to make me think somebody's coming behind me," Hedbirn sneered, "is much, much too old."

He held the pistol and silencer at arm's length, and shook it experimentally. He wished to be sure that the silencer was firm.

It was then that Morton brought his gun barrel down on Hedbirn's arm. A choppy, hard blow. Hedbirn dropped the pistol, silencer and all. Gasping, he dived for the guns on the table. But Morton pushed him, and he tumbled across that table and banged upon the floor.

"That's a nice position," said Morton, "Just hold it."

McGarvey whispered: "I—I still can't believe it."

"Get up," said Morton, "and start gathering cannons. You, Hedbirn, you stay where you are until we're ready for you."

He explained curtly. All he had wished to do at the hospital was blow himself to a nice long sleep, but soon after he got there he received a telephone report from the federal ballistics man, who had promised this; and he learned that the slug taken out of the stateroom wall didn't weigh enough to have been fired from an army .45. This confirmed a suspicion he had already formed. He hadn't believed that the gun found on the deck had recently been fired. It didn't smell that way. But what was it doing there?

"Slim and Hedbirn here must have had a scrap, and Slim lost his head and fired, missing. He used a .32 or a .35. He ran from the stateroom, stepped out on the deck for a second, and threw that gun overboard. Meanwhile, Hedbirn realized that there was bound to be an investigation of the shot, and he didn't want to be found with a gun himself because his own gun happened to be a stolen one. So he thought fast. One of his port holes was open. There weren't any others open along that part of the deck. From where he threw it, I suppose, he probably couldn't see the rail. But even if he heard it hit and fall back, it was too late then to do anything about it. He'd raised the alarm.

"At first I thought it was all an act to be sure there was a crowd of cops at the dock when we landed. Hedbirn must have been afraid somebody was laying for him there. But then I got to thinking about it, and I realized that if it had been prearranged between Slim and Hedbirn, Hedbirn certainly would have thrown that gun away first and not taken any chances the last minute with a port hole.

"At the hospital I got to worrying about you. I figured you'd be out getting yourself into trouble, as of course you were. I did a lot of work right there, through an extension phone they rigged up for me. I found out that Hedbirn's art business was mostly a fake. As he told you a little while ago, he couldn't stand an investigation, and once he was suspected he was sunk. It began to look more and more as though he was the center of this thing, to me.

"All the time I kept trying to locate you by telephone, and the reports I kept getting were worse and worse. You'd smacked down a cop in Ninth Avenue. You'd been seen hanging around a house where Slim Walkely was later found murdered, and you'd been seen coming out of that house. You didn't get back to your hotel, and didn't call there or leave any message. You'd rented an automobile. A guy exactly answering your description had assaulted a federal agent who was watching the drop where it seems Hedbirn kept his stock—he was watching it until a raiding squad could be collected, and when the raiders got there they found one dead gorilla and one with a nasty concussion.

"Well, what with one thing and another, it began to look as though you might be stumbling into the truth of the matter at last, in your own dumb way, before you even knew it yourself, and so I figured I'd better come here and head you off. The hospital people were nasty as hell about it, but I worked my pull with Martin and made them let me go.

"I let myself in here with a master key, and I'd just started snooping around when Hedbirn came in, so I hid in a bedroom closet. He was all excited about something, and started to pack fast. Then you came along."

MORTON GRINNED A little. He was facing his prisoner, but the grin was meant for McGarvey.

"I'd have stepped out sooner, and saved you some agony, only I wanted to hear what this bozo had to say for himself when he didn't know somebody else was listening."

McGarvey said: "We better get out of here."

"Why not wait for those two halfwits he talked about?"

"They're not coming, but maybe somebody else is! Walkely must have given Wallie Faben's brother this address and a good description of this guy. That's what he's so scared about."

Morton nodded.

"For once in your life, Garv, you're using your head. We'll march this bozo away and let Centre Street worry about Faben. They'll be glad to know he may show up here. They want him for lots of things."

Arthur Hedbirn wasn't the cold, emotionless slayer now. He could run through danger, he could even seek danger out, but he couldn't sit and wait for death to come. He didn't have that much nerve. He was silent, and seemed eager to depart. First Morton called Spring 7-3100.

"We're leaving," he finished that call, "but we'll leave the lights on, so if Faben and any of his boy friends show up they'll probably try to barge right in. I wouldn't fool around with them if I were you."

They went slowly out of the living room, down the entrance hall, Hedbirn in front, Morton and McGarvey close behind. Morton opened the door, McGarvey stepped out. Morton took Hedbirn's arm.

"You next, sweetheart."

But Hedbirn suddenly twisted away from him, spun on his heel and, bending low, dashed back into the living room.

"Well, of all the—"

Morton yelled: "Maybe he's got another gun there!"

It happened in less than thirty seconds. They reached the living room in time to see Hedbirn spring for the French windows. But one of those windows opened before he could get to it.

Then it was as though the whole penthouse exploded. One of the men standing in the window had eyes only for Arthur Hedbirn. He emptied the whole clip of his automatic at Hedbirn, and the distance wasn't more than a few feet. Hedbirn went backward as though kicked in the chest, but even after he hit the floor his body jerked again and again as the heavy bullets thunked into it.

The other man saw Morton and McGarvey. He vanished.

Max Faben had a second gun, but he was a little slow getting it out. The detectives both opened up on him at once.

He leaned against the window frame, smiling a little in spite of the blood which began to appear between his lips. He was looking at his brother's murderer as he slid to the floor, and he didn't seem to care about anything else.

McGarvey dashed for the window. Morton yelled at him.

"That other guy might be—"

McGarvey stood in the window, shooting. The runaway had reached the fire stairs, near the edge of the roof, but the door seemed stuck. He whirled, fired twice. He staggered backward, screamed; and then he just wasn't there any longer. They later found that one of McGarvey's bullets had hit him in the left shoulder. Which was pretty good work on the part of the physicians, in view of the condition of the body. The Besser is a twenty-two story building.

WHEN THE LAST flashlight had pommed, and the last reporter had shrieked his last question, and the train actually began to move, Wentworth L. Morton, who was getting old, sank back with a sigh, and swabbed at a perspiring forehead.

"Thank God *that's* over with! Though I suppose there'll be another army waiting for us at Philly. I wonder when that porter's going to bring the beer I ordered?"

McGarvey simply couldn't sit still. He kept looking at papers. His own likeness appeared many times in most of them. Morton's was there too, sometimes. But Morton wasn't much for posing. Again and again McGarvey had been obliged to haul him out in front of the cameras, for all the world like a concert singer noble-heartedly making her accompanist take a bow with her. Morton, the meanie! wouldn't consent to display his bandaged leg. Why the hell should he, he demanded, go pulling up his pants for the benefit of a lot of wild men?

"Boy! oh boy! That's what I call a send-off! Say, we got to fix it so's we can come back to this town some day. I didn't get half a chance to look at all the places I wanted to, with all those reporters and everybody hanging around. I never did see that Metropolitan Museum of Art, for instance," said McGarvey, who had never been to the art museum in Miami either, though he'd lived in that city all his life.

Morton was relaxed, and his eyes were closed. He said:

"You know, Garv, that crazy Irish luck of yours isn't going to hold out forever. Some one of these days, if you don't learn to stop and figure things out a little before you rush in, the way I keep telling you—"

"Look, Mort! It says here in this paper that step by step, all along the line of investigation, the Floridian sleuths— that's us, the Floridian sleuths—put all the best efforts of crack detectives of New York City and Washington to shame, cleaning up a bootleg firearms ring with national and possibly even international ramifications while other police officials were wholly in the dark."

"Oh, what can anybody do with a cluck like you! Shut up! I want to get some rest." Morton savagely jabbed the buzzer. "Where the hell do you suppose that porter is with my beer?"

"Mort, do you really think there will be some more of those newspaper guys waiting for us when we get to Philadelphia?"

McGARVEY FOLLOWS HIS NOSE

*Morton and McGarvey Go into the
Scavenging Business in Florida—and
What That Has to Do with a Bank Holdup
in Minnesota Is a Riddle for You*

McGARVEY LEANED OVER the back of the automobile seat, waving his arms awkwardly. Those arms were long and thick, and ended in huge hands. And McGarvey's large, boyish face was brick-red, which wasn't only because of the heat.

"There's no crooks in this town?" he insisted.

One of the men from St. Louis gave a twisted, tired smile.

"I always understood you had all modern improvements here," he said. "No crooks? Quite a place!"

The other man from St. Louis said, "Yeah, quite a place."

McGarvey's face flushed an even deeper red. He wasn't much more than a kid, and when he was rattled like this he blustered. His voice got louder.

"You say you tailed the guy this far—"

"He's here, somewhere."

"Why should a crook come to Miami in the summer?"

"I give up," one of the men from St. Louis said.

Morton sat in the front seat next to McGarvey, but he took no part in the talk. He was the best cop in Florida, twice McGarvey's age, and with ten times McGarvey's experience; and just now, because Captain Montgomery was on vacation, he was in charge of all city detectives.

The rat-faced fellow
swung the catsup bottle.

He looked like a weary bishop. He was gray and solid and thoughtful. He seldom smiled, and never laughed.

McGarvey shouted, "Well, we took you around, didn't we?"

"Sure. And it was very interesting. But we didn't find Finley."

"He isn't here, that's why! We got no crooks in this town ordinarily. Some local punks kick up a fuss now and then, maybe, but the only real trouble-makers are the guys who come from outside, in the season. Guys that come from places like St. Louis, for instance."

"Well, one of them's here now."

The visitors got out of the car. Morton got out, too, and solemnly shook hands with them.

"We'll see what we can do," Morton promised. "What hotel you boys going to use?"

"Gawd knows. You certainly got enough of them here. We'll give you a ring later, and let you know."

McGarvey, who hadn't stirred, and who had been glowering at the visitors, broke in:

"And I tell you you're wasting your time! There's no crime in this town except during the season! Why, it's so quiet around here this time of the year that—"

What interrupted him was a volley of gunfire which seemed to make the very pavement tremble, a screech of automobile tires, the high-pitched and prolonged screaming of a woman.

A touring car rocketed around the corner. In back of it was a police radio car. A cop in uniform was leaning out of the radio car, shooting. Somebody in the back seat of the touring car was shooting, too.

A front tire of the radio car blew with a terrific explosion, and the machine slewed across the opposite sidewalk and whammed into the door-way of a drug store. Glass crashed. The touring car passed a red light, missing other vehicles by mere inches.

Morton, gun out, jumped to the running board of the prowl car. McGarvey already was starting it, in second.

McGarvey could drive; nobody ever questioned that; and he knew the city perfectly. But there is never any accounting for pedestrians. A woman, fat and frightened, her face gleaming with perspiration, her arms filled with bundles—a woman who had been perfectly safe in a door-way when all the noise started—scampered into Miami Avenue like a panic-stricken hen. She didn't scream. She just put her head down and ran, as though convinced that only on the other side of the street could she find shelter.

McGarvey missed her. But in missing her he sideswiped an electric light pole, taking off the whole right fender and badly beading the front axle.

Morton had jumped. A second later Morton was on the running board of another car, and his gun still was in his right fist.

"After them!"

But this driver was a slow thinker, slower still to act.

McGarvey too, his chin cut by windshield glass, commandeered a car, and he had a little better luck with his driver, an excited boy.

But the touring car was out of sight by that time.

HALF AN HOUR later Morton and McGarvey, breathing heavily, went to the store where all this fuss had started. There was a big crowd outside. Inside, on the floor, an ambulance surgeon was leaning over one of the clerks.

"Maybe and maybe not," the ambulance surgeon said, without looking up. "I won't make any promises. The very least he's got is a nasty concussion."

There was another clerk. He had been slugged, too; but now he was becoming coherent.

"One of them walks up to where I'm standing and asks could he look at some neckties, and I start to open the showcase, and the next thing I know he's pressing a cannon against my guts and telling me to walk to the back. I'd have gone. I'm no fool! In fact, I was starting back there when Joey began to give the other man an argument. I don't know what got into him. He's a quiet guy ordinarily. Anyway, that other man slugged him something terrible! I couldn't stand it, and I was starting to yell when this man in front of me smacked me over the ear. I guess he must have used his gun. It felt like that."

"Knock you out?"

"Not exactly. Anyway, I didn't fall down. But I couldn't have been really conscious, I guess. I saw them clean out the cash register, but I couldn't seem to do anything but lean there and watch them. And then, when they went outside, those radio cops came along and all the shooting started."

The two detectives from St. Louis had drifted into the store, unnoticed. One of them said to the other:

"Nice quiet town, isn't it?"

"Yeah," said the other. "It's a cinch to see they don't ever have any crooks here in the summertime."

2

AT THE END of the day the detective force of Miami had got nowhere. A general alarm had been sent out. Dozens of witnesses had given dozens of different descriptions of the two holdup men. The car in which they escaped had been found abandoned in Coconut Grove, and was identified; it belonged to a man who was sipping a soda in a Coral Gables drug store, and who didn't even know, until the cops told him, that it had been stolen. And Joey Raymond, the haberdashery clerk, had died of a fractured skull.

Young McGarvey walked up and down the office, waving his arms.

"Turn me loose on some of the punks in this town, Mort, and I'll soon find out who it was pulled that job!"

For McGarvey was a strongarm squad in himself. He liked that kind of work. He wasn't too brainy perhaps, but he stood six feet three, and weighed two hundred and thirty pounds, and he didn't know the meaning of fear.

Sergeant Morton shook his head. Morton never seemed to hurry about anything; and except when he was calling down his partner, like a stern parent restraining a youngster, he never raised his voice.

"No," Morton said. "Those boys weren't local. They're too good. They picked an inconspicuous car. They stole it without even touching the ignition key. They used their heads when a clerk got resisty, and instead of shooting him they slugged him. They slugged the other man, too. And even then they were cool enough to rifle the cash register before they went out. When the patrol happened to spot them they did some very nifty driving and some nifty shooting—and got away. It was a small-time job, maybe, but it was done in a big-time manner by red-hots, not heels.

"So what? Certainly one of them wasn't this guy Finley?"

"Oh, no. Finley's a confidence man and a swindler. He wouldn't go in for rough stuff like that."

"I think it was home talent! You let me go out and do a little asking the way I like—"

"No. Maybe sometimes that stuff's all right, but it wouldn't get us anywhere in this case." Morton stared out the window. "Another thing. Those St. Louis dicks aren't the only ones that have told us somebody's hanging out here. Remember that wire from New York last week? Remember Havana asking us to pick up a murderer who'd been seen here? And we couldn't find him?"

"That doesn't mean the guys are still around! They might have just gone through."

"They might. But have you noticed how many federals there are in Miami these past few days? They've been coming here quietly from Jacksonville and Atlanta and even from Washington. You can't get anything out of them about what they're doing here, but it certainly isn't going to be a convention."

"A lot of Boy Scouts!"

"Maybe. But they've pulled some swell arrests lately, those F.B.I. men. And when there's as many of them as this in one place you can be pretty sure they're not looking

for somebody who's wanted for traffic violations or spitting
on the sidewalk."

Morton got up, carefully put on a Panama.

"No, Garv. There's a cooling-off plant in this town somewhere, and I guess we'd better find it."

"What are you going to do now?"

Morton shrugged. "Follow my nose, I guess. That's as
good a system as any."

"And what about my putting on a little heat?"

Morton sighed. An inherently secretive man, he
preferred to work alone. His partner was handy to have
around in case of a fight, but not otherwise notably useful.
Morton tolerated him because he liked the kid, and
because he had liked McGarvey's father, for many years
his sidekick. The old man had been another of those loud-
mouthed, aggressive, fearless Irishmen. He would flounder
into anything, bellowing. He had floundered into a flock
of lead one night in a roadhouse, with Morton at his side.
They still talked about that gun battle, which had sent
Morton to the hospital for three months and McGarvey,
Sr., to his grave. It was largely because of this, and the wave
of sentimentality which followed it, that young McGarvey
had been elevated to the detective division. The kid was
much too young for the job, in every respect.

"All right," Morton said. "But try not to kill anybody."

McGarvey swung out of the office like an escaped tiger
returning to the jungle.

WENTWORTH L. MORTON wandered about the city
for more than three hours. Quietly, amiably, looking like
anything in the world but a celebrated sleuth on the trail
of desperate gangsters, he went about chatting with hotel

men, garage men, service station men. He asked questions which were seemingly idle, and got the sort of answers he might have expected—until he talked with the proprietor of a tourist home in Southwest Eighth Street.

"Funny thing," this man said. "Most of us guys are starving, and yet the other night there was a party in here that said they'd actually got turned away from one place."

"That is funny," Morton agreed. His face held no expression. "Where was this place, did they say?"

"Somewhere out around Twenty-Sixth or Twenty-Seventh. This party'd come from the West Coast, and they'd got lost, and they stopped at the first 'Tourist' sign they happened to see. There's another funny thing: Here we got a swell location, right on the Trail, and we're empty; and yet a place nobody ever heard of, that's on a side street, is turning 'em away."

"You don't know the name of this place, do you?"

"No, I don't. These people didn't say."

Morton ceased wandering. He went to the home of a friend, a man who was out of a job. He got this friend, and his wife and two children, and three suitcases, to visit tourist homes in Twenty-Sixth and Twenty-Seventh avenues. They tried seven places. In the first six they were promptly and gladly offered accommodations, but they found some fault with each and went away. In the seventh they were told there was no vacancy. Thereafter they went to police headquarters where the man reported to his friend Sergeant Morton, who thanked him, gave him a five-dollar bill, and warned him to keep his mouth shut.

Then Morton went looking for his partner.

Following young McGarvey was easy enough. Morton

went from complaint to complaint. Here a drinking place, there a poolroom, or a small restaurant, or a private poker game. McGarvey had been mussing 'em up, and they weren't happy. One man had a front tooth out; another was putting beefsteak on his left eye.

"Say call that gorilla of yours off, won't you! We told him we don't know a thing about that stickup, but he wouldn't believe us!"

"Do you good to get pushed around a little every now and then," Morton said negligently. "Show you your place."

"Yeah? Well, if that lummox keeps on doing that sort of stuff—"

"Never mind about McGarvey. He knows his business."

It was in a little chile joint in Biscayne Boulevard that Morton caught up to him. McGarvey was at the far end of the counter. He had a street corner sport by the lapels, and was shaking him. The proprietor looked worried. The only other person in the place, a thin, rat-faced fellow, already had been questioned. He was standing directly behind McGarvey, glowering at McGarvey's back and nursing a sore chin.

Nobody noticed Morton, who entered silently, hands in pockets.

"Now never mind that bunk. What I want to know is what guys was it pulled that Flagler Street job this afternoon?"

The rat-faced fellow took a catsup bottle from the counter. His patience was at an end. He swung the bottle, went up on his toes.

Morton, without even taking his hands out of his pockets, gave Rat-Face a terrific kick in the pants. It almost knocked Rat-Face off his feet. He dropped the bottle, which smashed on the tile floor.

McGarvey wheeled.

"What's this? Were you trying to crown me, you little—"

"All right," Morton cut in. "Forget it, Garv! You've had your little fun, and now it's time to go to work."

"What do you think I been doing? I haven't found out much—"

"Well, I have," said Morton. "Come on."

In the car he told McGarvey about the Hotel Adelbert. The big fellow's reaction was prompt, and entirely typical.

"Well, we walk into the joint and grab the manager and shake his guts loose until he tells us who he's got there."

"And get ourselves killed? Suppose there's a whole army of fugitives in that place? It's licensed to accommodate thirty guests."

"Well, we'll take a squad! We'll surround the place!"

"And then find out that there's nothing wrong with it after all. And make damn fools of ourselves? You can't call out a squad without calling out the reporters too."

"Well, then, what *are* we going to do about it?" McGarvey demanded morosely.

"We're going to move into the house across the street, which happens to be for rent furnished. I've fixed it up already. After that we just do some watching. So you pack a suitcase."

3

—

IT WAS NOT McGarvey's idea of detective work, this business of just sitting there, hour after weary hour, watching the front of the Hotel Adelbert, which was a no-account, three-story stucco building.

If the Adelbert actually contained the thirty guests it was licensed to accommodate, they certainly kept quiet. The place looked deserted. Nobody ever appeared at the front door, or in the bare backyard, or in the garage. Nobody even appeared at the windows.

The shades were all drawn. There were four brittle, dirty, cane rockers on the front porch, but they were never used. Yet the milkman left a full dozen bottles there, and earlier a newsboy threw a paper on the porch. A grocery truck stopped there, a butcher's truck, a bakery wagon. These delivery cars went up the little drive to the side door, and somebody appeared at that door to accept the goods. Morton and McGarvey could not see who it was who appeared.

"The license is made out to a man named Anton Schultz," Morton reported.

McGarvey sat in a Morris chair, at a front window. He was scowling, a mountain of impatience. Slouched as he was, he could see under the shade, which was lowered to a point only about two inches above the window sill. There was an automatic rifle across his knees.

"How 'bout tapping the telephone wire?"

"I've arranged for that. But I doubt whether it's going to get us very far. Except that they seem to be ordering plenty of food."

"I don't see how *this* is going to get us very far, either, if it comes to that! What we ought to do is crash the place!"

"First I want to find out who's in there," Morton said.

"And how in hell do you expect to do that?"

Morton was making himself a highball. His partner's petulance didn't worry him. He was used to it.

"You notice the garbage truck that came a little while ago?"

"What's that got to do with it?"

"Those two garbage men are working under my orders. They drove around to the side door, where the two barrels were, and the one on the ground picked up those barrels and carried them around to the other side of the truck. He tossed a couple of barrels up to the man in the truck, who emptied them and tossed them back."

"Well, naturally."

"But they weren't the same barrels. They were a couple that looked just about the same, only they'd been fastened to that ledge on the other side of the truck, so that they couldn't be seen from the hotel. What the garbage man did was simply take the barrels from the hotel and fasten them to that ledge, still full, and put the two empty barrels back. And he drove off with the full barrels."

"What's the idea of all that?"

"Because I want to examine that garbage. And now that

it's getting dark the man ought to be bringing it here, to the back door, by coming through the back yard of the house behind us. In fact, that sounds like him now."

Morton went out. Young McGarvey started after him, shaking his huge head. You never could tell what old Mort was going to do next. And what was still worse, you never knew what he was thinking. He kept things to himself. Which sometimes made McGarvey feel like an awkward kid, and sometimes made him sore. This time he was sore.

After a while utter darkness settled in the room. McGarvey's nose began to twitch, and he frowned a deeper frown. He rose, ambled back into the kitchen.

"Most of the windows are lighted over there," he reported. "It looks like—"

He stopped. Wentworth L. Morton, a fresh highball in his fist, was ankle-deep in empty tin cans, potato peelings, carrot tops, corn cobs, scraps of paper, pieces of string, broken glass, empty liquor and beer bottles, grease-covered bones, egg shells, cigar butts, coffee grounds....

"This is very interesting," Morton said, nodding.

"It's very smelly! My God, if being a detective means being a scavenger, I'm not sure I'm glad I joined the force."

"Sometimes you have to do a lot of things, when you're a cop."

"But you stink, Mort! The whole place stinks!"

Morton finished his highball, got down on his hands and knees.

"What are you looking for, anyway?" McGarvey asked.

"I don't know," said Morton. "I'm just looking."

"Just following your nose, huh?"

"That's the idea."

McGarvey stamped back to the front room. He threw himself into the Morris chair and fixed a prolonged dirty look upon the innocent-looking Hotel Adelbert across the street.

Three days later the situation, to all appearances, was unchanged. McGarvey still fumed, asking why they didn't just go across the street and barge into that dump and demand to know who lived there. And Morton still moved gravely from place to place, sometimes relieving McGarvey at the Morris chair, more often telephoning or reading books or examining papers. Morton was a great one for work.

"There's about twelve or thirteen men over there," he announced, the third night.

"How do you know that? From the food they've ordered?"

"Partly. But mostly from the garbage. The scavengers were around again today, and they just delivered another two cans out back."

"So I noticed when you came in the room. You smell terrible."

"They might order groceries a little ahead, maybe expecting more guests or something, but they'd only eat just so much each day. Twelve or thirteen, I estimate."

"A lot of no-account punks, scared out of their wits!"

"I wonder," said Morton.

He was reading a copy of Lockwood's "Directory of the Paper and Allied Trades," and marking the lines with a telegram which had come to him an hour earlier. He had received several telegrams in these three days, and scores of telephone calls. Three times boys had called for small packages, which Morton gave them. But Morton was characteristically secretive about all this; and McGarvey, being sore, and disgusted, didn't like to ask questions.

"You might at least get another guy here to help us watch," McGarvey grumbled. "Two of us to keep staring out this damn window twenty-four hours a day is getting hard on the eyes."

"Yes, I'll call headquarters and have them send somebody. I don't want to have too much activity going on here, but it wouldn't do any harm now, I think, to have another man."

"Ask 'em to send somebody who knows his way around in a kitchen. You're a swell cop, Mort, but you certainly are a rotten cook. Besides, you stink. I suppose that garbage is all over the kitchen floor again?"

"Yes." Morton sighed, reaching for the telephone. "Yes, I'm afraid it is."

"If this keeps up much longer, I'm going to bust the case myself by just going over there and walking into that place!"

Morton only smiled.

THE FOLLOWING DAY Captain Montgomery came back from his vacation, a week early, and Morton talked with him over the telephone for a long time. Late in the afternoon Montgomery and two plainclothesmen called in person. McGarvey was in the front room, sullenly staring out under the lowered shade, and with him was the relief man, Majors. Sergeant Morton conducted the visitors to the kitchen.

"Lovely place," said Montgomery, holding his nose.

"You get used to it," Morton assured him. "Now tell me what you've fixed?"

"Well, I got seventeen men altogether. Two down at each end of this block that'll stop all traffic as soon as I give the word. Four in the block back of the hotel there, mostly hiding in bushes around the different houses. Two in each of the houses on each side of this one. Three in that house to the left of the hotel there, and two more in that clump of hibiscus over on the right. And besides that, there's six of us in here now.

"Three of the boys have got submachine guns, and four have automatic rifles. Three of them have tear gas bombs. In addition to all that, there's three cars without any department insignia, all hanging around within whistling distance."

"Swell," Morton said. "You didn't tip off the federals?"

"No, because, like you said over the phone, there's no reason to ring them in on it and give them a chance to grab all the glory."

Montgomery was troubled. He was a good administrator, a good politician, but it was Morton who, in emergencies, really ran the detective division. For Montgomery was shrewd enough to realize that Morton had more brains than all the rest of the department put together. He relied upon Morton, trusted him. Nevertheless he was troubled now.

"That's a hell of a big squad, Mort. Are you sure of this thing? I know you like to work by yourself and all that, and I don't ordinarily interfere with you, do I? But I can't help thinking you ought to tell us what makes you believe there's a volcano in that place."

"All right," Morton said, unexpectedly. He motioned to the garbage with which the floor was strewn. "In that stuff the day before yesterday there was a little triangle of paper which I haven't got here now. It was yellow, and looked like bank paper. Just a piece not much bigger than your thumb print. No writing or printing on it, and no trace of a watermark. I borrowed a micrometer caliper with a rachet stop from a friend of mine and found out the paper was ninety-two one-thousands of an inch thick—which is pretty thin for that kind of stuff.

"So I got in touch with Sanderson, the paper expert in Jacksonville, by long distance, and he told me it sounded as if it might be a chunk of one of the blank checks stolen in that Northern Minnesota Trust stickup last month in St. Paul. You remember that one? Where a teller was machine-gunned?"

Montgomery exclaimed, "That was Al Koppinger's gang did that! Do you suppose *those* guys could be across the street?"

"They just grabbed everything in sight," Morton pursued quietly, "and one of the things they grabbed was a big batch of check paper which hadn't been bound up into books yet. Most of that was found later, thrown away, when their hideout was raided. But a couple of checks had been torn out. Maybe somebody in the gang figured on using them for note paper, or maybe they had some idea of flying a kite on that bank later. It was a dumb thing to do, in any case.

"Well, I sent that scrap of paper up to Sanderson by air mail, which is why I haven't got it here now. But in the meanwhile, before he could get it and examine it and phone me a report, I found another piece of the same kind of paper in today's batch of garbage. I can't be sure of the thickness because there's a film of grease on this piece, but I took a tracing of the other one, and the edge of this one matches that tracing perfectly. Here it is."

He produced a scrap of paper not more than three inches long and half an inch wide. He held it up to the light.

In this one there's a little of the watermark, see? Gothic capitals. An 'S' and a 'T' and the beginning of what must be an 'A.' Well, I looked that up in Lockwood's 'Directory.' The whole watermark would be 'Garden State Bond,' and it's made by a firm in Newark, New Jersey.

"I called them direct, because there's a little slur on the bottom of that 'T' that looks like it was made by a defectively soldered wire on the dandy-roll. That's the kind of thing that might happen any time, but they usually find it pretty fast and fix it. Doesn't do the paper any harm, of course, but it makes it much easier to identify.

"Well, the Newark people were all excited, because it seems the Bureau of Investigation experts from Washington had been there asking them about the same thing a little while before. They'd only turned out a small lot of that paper before they discovered the chipped wire on the dandy-roll, and fixed it. And every bit of that paper had gone to the Northern Minnesota Trust and had been stolen by the Koppinger gang. That was why the federals were tracing it.

"So there you are," Morton said mildly, putting down the paper and a magnifying glass. "That ought to be enough to stage a raid on, shouldn't it?"

"I'LL SAY SO! Why, Al Koppinger rates as Number One,

and they've been looking for his gang for the past two months!" said Montgomery.

"And all the time," said Morton, "they were in that cooling-off plant across the street, which is the last place in the world they expected anybody to be looking for them. I expect there's a lot of other hot boys there too. Some of them got bored the other day and decided to take a little local flyer just to relieve the monotony. So they knocked over a haberdashery."

"Let's go," said Montgomery, "before it begins to get dark."

"I'll go up and tell Garv and Majors," Morton said. "Garv thinks there's nothing but a few drug store tinhorns in that place, and he's been sitting around biting his fingernails and just dying for some action."

"It's a wonder he hasn't walked out on you and gone right over."

"He's threatened to. But you know Garv. His old man all over again."

Majors came out of the front room. He was a young fellow, recently out of harness, and not sure of himself. He looked from Morton to Montgomery and back. He waved his hands.

"Say, I don't know what I could have done. I had no authority to stop the guy."

"What are you talking about?"

"Why, young McGarvey. He hadn't said a word for at least an hour, and just now he gets up all of a sudden and announces that he's going to end this business of sitting around getting nowhere. He said he was going right across the street and into that hotel. And he just went out the front door. What could I do? I couldn't stop him without getting him shot—"

Morton raced to the front window. The front door of the Hotel Adelbert was ajar, but there was nobody in sight.

"That crazy kid!" Montgomery cried. "He'll spoil everything! He'll start trying to smack somebody, and they'll jump him! And when they realize the place's surrounded they'll hold him as a hostage and walk him out at the point of a gun, so's we won't dare take a shot at them!"

Morton said nothing. He was staring out the window. Of course, it was the kid's own fault... But still....

"They'll get away! Here we got the Koppinger gang all wrapped up and because of that overgrown galoot they'll walk away from us! Every cop in the country will be giving us the merry ha-ha!"

Morton said slowly, "Never mind about the merry ha-ha. We got to get him out of there."

"If we rush the place—"

"If we rush the place we'll only lose a lot of other men, besides Garv." Morton shook his head. "There's only one thing to do. I'm going to go there, quietly. Don't send anybody after me, and don't make a move at least until you hear artillery, understand?"

"Say, listen, Mort: I can't let you walk into a place like—"

"*You* can't let me? You'll keep your trap shut and do what I say!" This wasn't an old and cautious man now. Mort's blue-gray eyes flashed, and his nostrils were squeezed tight. He stuck a stumpy forefinger under the nose of his superior officer. "Who's running this job? Who found this place? Who identified that paper? As far as I'm concerned, Monty, you're still on vacation!"

He went through the kitchen, kicking garbage, and snatched a small suitcase. He went out the back door.

A little later the men at the window saw him coming along the street, on the other side. He had cut through the block in back, and was walking around. He seemed tired, and very hot. He was carrying the suitcase.

In front of the Hotel Adelbert he stopped, wiped his face with a handkerchief, exhaled heavily.

There was nobody else in sight, and the hum of traffic from Southwest Eighth Street, which is a through highway, was faint. Full sunlight still held the land, though the shadows were getting long. There was not any indication that men with guns were watching, on all sides. The air was heavy, damp. The palmettos with which the short walk to the Adelbert porch was lined had drooped hot and dry, a little brown at the edges, and motionless.

Morton glanced at the "Tourist" sign. It seemed to give him an idea. He shrugged—and walked into the hotel.

"God help him," Captain Montgomery whispered. "He's got more guts than I'll ever have."

4

IT WAS DIM in the lobby. Dim and bare. A few overstuffed chairs were there, and a desk and a bell and a telephone. There wasn't much more—except a man behind the desk.

He had a thick Germanic face, bright with perspiration. His heavy mustache, dark brown, sagged sadly. His eyes were little. Before Morton could speak this man tapped the hand bell.

Morton limped a little as he crossed the lobby. When he was tired he always limped. His right leg had been broken when Old Man McGarvey was blasted out, in that night club battle.

"Got room for a guy for the night?"

The Germanic man said, "No."

Morton dropped his suitcase, wiped his face again.

"I'm tired! You mean to say I got to walk further?"

"That's right. We're full up here."

Morton sighed, and dropped into a chair, and his head sank back.

"Mind if I rest here for a while? I'm all worn out."

The Germanic one looked angry, but uncertain. A door at the end of the desk opened, and another man appeared. This was a very tall man, rangy, with a long, hard, heavily-tanned face.

"How'd you happen to come in here?" the German asked.

"Huh?" Morton looked up. His eyelids were heavy like those of a man fighting off sleep. He shook his head as though to clear it. "Oh, yes… A guy told me about you. Guy I used to know in stir."

"Yeah? Who would he be?"

The tall man said nothing. He didn't like Morton's looks.

"I got his note here somewheres," Morton said, and fumbled in a coat pocket. Presently he withdrew a slip of paper, started to unfold it. "Here you are." He didn't get out of the chair.

The Germanic one came around from behind the desk. The tall man moved with him. They stood on either side of Morton.

The paper, as it happened, was a note scribbled on the back of a police form by McGarvey. Morton had found it under his telephone, a week or so ago. Now he held the printed side down so that only the pencil writing showed. The German reached for it.

"Let's see—"

Morton was out of that chair in one swift leap, like a caged boxer bounding away from the ropes. He hit the tall man twice, with the barrel of his gun. He twisted, stooping.

"Hold it!"

The German had dropped the note. His right hand had gone under his coat. But now, facing Morton, he was paralyzed.

The tall man was on the floor, and there was blood trickling from a cut over his left ear.

Morton said, very quietly, "Take your hand away from there, Schultz. And take it away slowly, with the fingers out stiff."

Schultz obeyed. He knew better than to fool with a man who looked at him the way Morton did. At Morton's command he raised his hands shoulder-high and turned his back. Morton took his gun.

"There's a guy came in here a little while ago," Morton said. "He's a big guy, and young, with an Irish face. What'd you do with him?"

"I don't know what you're talking about...."

"I tell you: What did you do with him?"

"I swear I don't know what—what was that?"

The tall man had stirred, moaned a little, and Morton, bending his knees, had deliberately hit him again in the same place. Morton hated to do a thing like that. He disliked violence.

"That was your pal," Morton purred, "and he got what you're going to get pretty soon, unless you tell me where that kid is."

"What is this, anyway? A stickup?" Morton jammed the gun muzzle very hard into Schultz's back, causing Schultz to grunt sharply and rock forward on the balls of his feet.

"I haven't got time to argue with you, Schultz! *Talk!*"

"Listen, I tell you I don't know what—"

From behind Morton somebody said:

"You better put that thing down, buddy, before you get hurt."

MORTON TURNED ONLY his head, and he turned that very slowly. He sensed, even before he saw the two men in the doorway, that any quick movement would mean his death. The two men were strangers to him. Neither was Al Koppinger, whose likeness had been conspicuous in every police station, sheriff's office and post office in the country for the past two months. But they might be associates of Koppinger.

They were standing in the doorway through which the tall man had come. One aimed a heavy automatic. The other held, at his hip, a sub-machine gun.

The second man said lazily, "Schultz might get it too, buddy, but that wouldn't help you out any. Now drop that gat and be nice."

Morton dropped his gun. Schultz, the instant he heard it fall, whirled around and punched Morton twice in the mouth. His little brown eyes were blazing, and under the brown mustache his mouth twitched. Morton didn't move.

"Cut it out, Schultz," one of the men said.

Schultz hit Morton again, this time to the left cheek. Still Morton did not move. The man with the automatic went over to Schultz, grabbed him by the shoulder, hauled him away. The other man stood at a safe distance, his machine gun always pointed at Morton.

"Tell us what it's all about, buddy. I'm curious."

"I came in here looking for a friend of mine." Morton's speech was thick because of the blood on his lips. He licked the blood away, but more kept gushing out.

"Is this the way you look for friends in this town?"

Morton didn't answer.

The man with the machine gun jerked his head toward the door.

"Outside, Schultz, and look!"

Schultz first recovered his pistol, roughing Morton as he did so. He went out the front door, muttering all the time.

After that there was a long silence. The two men stood looking at Morton, and Morton looked at the floor, and nothing stirred. The world might have come to an end, as far as that lobby was concerned. Nobody paid any attention to the man on the floor.

When Schultz returned he said, "I went all around and I couldn't see anybody at all. But just the same, I had a feeling that somebody was watching me."

"Yeah," said the man with the machine gun. "I kind of have that same feeling. We'd better go upstairs." They went to the third floor. The corridor was long, and the doors opening upon it looked alike. Schultz knocked four times at the door nearest the front, on the left. Then he knocked again. Something clicked, and Schultz turned the handle and pushed open the door.

Al Koppinger, small and extraordinarily pale, with snake-like black eyes, was waiting there. He had an automatic in each hand. His eyes caught Morton instantly, and he seemed to be unaware of anybody else.

"Well, well, well," he said softly. "A cop huh? I'd know one a mile away. Come right in, sweetheart."

5

IT GOT SO, after a while, that it didn't hurt. Waves of pain passed over Morton regularly, but monotonously, slowly; and after the first furious burn and sting they came to be almost soothing. For these fools didn't even know how to beat a man properly. Morton was only half conscious, almost from the beginning.

He lay in the middle of the floor, and they hit him with the butts of pistols and kicked him until they were tired. He didn't make a sound.

In fact, the whole business was uncommonly quiet. Schultz stayed at the window, gazing down at the discouraged palmettos in front. Al Koppinger leaned over Morton, slapping Morton's face with a pistol barrel, and asking questions in a low voice.

"You got anybody with you, copper? Anybody know you're here?"

Morton could hear him, and could hear the others panting and sometimes talking, but he made no answer.

Schultz, from the window, said, "Somebody really ought to go down and see after Wes. He took an awful clout from this shamus."

"The hell with Wes!" one of the men panted. "We got to crack this baby fast, or there may be the hottest kind of trouble!"

"He said something to Schultz about having a friend here."

"That was baloney. He was just saying it for an excuse to look around. You can see from the stuff we took from him he's a cop."

These voices Morton could hear, though they were blurred and meaningless. But the only thing he could feel, now, was a brutal, throbbing pain in his right leg just below the knee. That was where the leg had been broken by a bullet, a year and a half ago.

"There's no sense slugging this guy any more." Al Koppinger straightened. "He can take just about anything, I guess. And we'll have him out of the picture pretty soon, where he won't do us any good." He examined the articles taken from Morton's pockets. "But I'll tell you what: according to these papers this guy is Sergeant Morton, who's supposed to be the smartest cop in the state."

"That smart cop stuff is all newspaper drool! He probably knows a lot of reporters, and they play him up when there's no real news."

"Well, whether it's drool or not," Koppinger said, "this guy's a big hero around here and they all like him. All right. Suppose the joint is surrounded? We'll walk out with this guy in front of us, and with a Tommy sticking into his back where everybody can see it. Do you suppose they're going to let fly at us then?"

"Where'll we go?"

"To the car, of course. The door's open. We'll just get in and take this guy along with us. And we'll blow out of town. They won't dare to try to stop us when they know we've got Morton."

"Then what'll we do with him if we do get clear?"

Al Koppinger smiled, and looked at the ceiling.

"Oh, I can think of a lot of things," he answered.

"We blow, and what happens to the rest of my guests here? Finley and those others?" Schultz cried.

"We don't care what happens to them," Koppinger said cheerfully, "so long as they keep out of our way. And they'll do that all right. Guys in this dump stick to their own rooms."

"Say, I'm taking in almost half a grand a week from this hotel and I don't want to—"

Koppinger said, smoothly, "Would you rather get what Morton here's going to get?"

Schultz was silent. He had not moved from the window. Koppinger smiled meaningly at him for a moment, and then bent over Morton.

"Open the door, Patsy. We'll make this guy walk somehow."

He started to tug at Morton's shoulders. One of the men opened the hall door.

And young McGarvey charged into the room.

It was perfectly timed, almost like a mechanical stunt. Maybe something electrical. The door was opened—and McGarvey bounded in. Just like that.

But the instant afterward all hell broke loose.

McGarvey had a gun in each hand, and he didn't stop to ask questions. He didn't stoop, he didn't try to get behind anything. He just waded in, legs apart, blazing away right and left, and roaring like a steam engine.

The man with the machine gun jerked it up, and then dropped it and went right over backward as though he'd been kicked in the chest. As a matter of fact, they found out later that a .45 slug smashed his breastbone.

The second man fired once, but only once. Then his knees buckled, and he slid to the floor. McGarvey shot him twice more as he fell.

Al Koppinger had to reach for his hardware, but he was crouching, and McGarvey had not fired at him because McGarvey was afraid of hitting Morton. Koppinger's right hand disappeared, came in sight again with an automatic. He fired once at McGarvey. Before he had a chance to fire again Morton had grabbed his ankle and pulled hard. Koppinger went over backward, shrieking. The gun exploded twice, but the shots were wild.

McGarvey, by now, was on his knees. One arm hung limp, but there still was a pistol in the other hand, and McGarvey emptied this into Public Enemy Number One.

Schultz had jumped out the window. Probably he thought a whole raiding squad was entering the room and hoped to land safely on the roof of the front porch. Anyway, he kicked out the screen—the window was open—and threw a leg over the sill. The boys outside, across the street, could scarcely be blamed for what followed. They had been fingering triggers, and straining their eyes and ears, for more than half an hour, and every one of them was in an agony of suspense, knowing that both Morton and McGarvey were in that building. So when they heard the shooting and saw Schultz trying an exit—

It sounded as if the whole block had been dynamited, the way miners sometimes blast the whole side of a hill. Schultz was a much heavier man when he hit that porch roof. They took twenty-six pieces of lead out of him afterwards, at the autopsy.

YOUNG McGARVEY MOVED his head. He could do that without pain—which was more than the sergeant in the next bed could do. McGarvey's left leg and his right arm were in casts, but he could move his head—and grin.

"And all the time I thought it was just going to be a matter of pushing around a few local punks! It was funny, having desperados like that in this town in the summertime."

"Yeah," said Wentworth L. Morton. "Yeah, it was a scream."

"You might know they'd be out-of-towners! If only those other cities would stop sending gangsters down here we'd have a nice, quiet, law-abiding town!"

"And then what would you do?" Morton wet his lips. He did even that carefully, because the lips hurt. "You know, Garv, I thought all the time you'd done what you said you would—walked right into that place by the front door."

"Hell, I'm not as dumb as all that!"

Morton said dubiously, "Well, you're pretty dumb...."

"But not as bad as *that!* What I did was slip onto the running board of a grocery truck that was just going up to that side door. The driver didn't see me, and of course the guy who came to the side door didn't see me. Then when the truck backed out I slipped into the building through one of the cellar windows. And I started to prowl.

"The way I found out you had come in after me was because when I got to the lobby I found a tall guy who'd been socked, and he was just coming to. I made him tell me what happened, and I took his gun, and then I socked him again to keep him quiet. I was going to the front door and whistle for Majors or Monty or somebody—I didn't know there was a whole array out there—but something told me maybe the front was being watched from above."

"It was. I'd have been put out right off the bat, if you'd done that."

"Yeah. Well, so what I did was to go prowling again, looking for you."

"But what I can't understand is this," Morton said, frowning at the ceiling. "How did you find out where I was? All those doors on the second and third floors looked just the same, and the guys didn't make any noise when they were working over me. And yet when they opened the door of the room, there you were, you half-witted ape! all posed to take a flyer and smash that door in. How'd you know I was in there, anyway?"

McGarvey grinned.

"I just did what you've told me to. You say: When in doubt, follow your nose. Which was what I did. I went sniffing."

"You followed—"

"Nobody could smell as bad as that and not be you. You and all your garbage! As a matter of fact, Mort, you *still* stink!"

MURDER FOR ART'S SAKE

In the Depths of a Florida Swamp
Morton and McGarvey Find a Strange
and Priceless Motive for Murder

1

THREE SHOTS AT NIGHT

McGARVEY HAPPENED TO be near the switchboard and he plugged in. A moment later he was at the door of the office he shared with Wentworth L. Morton. Morton, as usual, was working.

McGarvey yelled, "*Hot* dawg! Bayshore Drive, out near the airport!"

Then he was off, excited as a kid running to a fire.

Morton ran after him. Somehow Morton never seemed to hurry—it was his dignity—yet he could move fast enough on emergency calls. He was a man of average stature, rather thick across the chest, and solid, but he looked a Singer midget alongside of his young partner, who was six feet three and weighed some two hundred and forty pounds, none of which was fat.

When he reached the car McGarvey was already behind the wheel and had the engine going. They started with a jerk, in second.

"Make that siren work!"

Morton said wearily, "You love that thing, don't you?" But he turned the siren. It was safest when McGarvey drove. He was a swell driver, McGarvey; but in order to ride with him at a time like this, and not have your hair turn white, you needed nerves of the sort Wentworth L. Morton had.

Well, they didn't hit anything, though there were moments when even Morton thought that all was over. McGarvey shot out a long arm and swung sharply left without slackening speed. They did that turn on two wheels. They slashed up a gravel drive between rows of date palms, and screeched to a stop in front of the home of Elias March.

"Murders and assaults," panted Morton as he climbed out, "are always an anticlimax after riding there with you."

The two radio patrol cops had arrived a minute and a half earlier. They were on the porch talking to Elias March.

One of them said, "He says nothing wrong at all, Mort."

"What is this?" McGarvey blustered. "What's happened here?"

Elias March was an all-year resident; old, a bachelor, a crank, reputedly rich. Nobody knew much about him, except that he could make a lot of trouble when he felt like it. Now he wore a heavy flannel bathrobe which made him look like a pipeless Sherlock Holmes. He had a Holmesian face too, long and saturnine.

"That's what *I* want to know: what is this?" he snapped. "What in the world's the matter with all you fools?"

Morton made the top step, paused an instant, to catch his breath, and then said apologetically:

"Somebody telephoned police headquarters, Mr. March, that a shot was heard in this house and that they saw three men run down the drive and get into a car." He turned to the radio patrol cops. "Incidentally, get busy. It's supposed

Morton, through the open window, shot him in the right arm.

to be a large touring car, some dark color, and at least four men in it. There was one at the wheel."

The patrol cops raced away.

Elias March spluttered, "See here! Now see here! What in the world do you mean by pounding in here like this! Get out of here!"

"Wait a minute," said McGarvey, and pushed past the old man and into the living room. "We came here to find out what the shooting was about, see? Well, what was it?"

"See here! I've told you there wasn't anything at all happened here, and you're absolutely crazy! Or *somebody* is!"

"Now wait a minute," said McGarvey. "What we came here for—"

Old March, almost as tall as the rookie detective, but not half his weight, would have hit him. Morton grabbed his partner's arm.

"Say, this guy can't—"

Morton said, "Shut up, Garv. I'll handle this."

WHEN McGARVEY GOT excited he blustered and bullied. He wasn't naturally that way. He was the most good-natured fellow in the world, ordinarily. But when he got excited only Morton, more than twice his age, could quiet him.

Morton addressed the owner of the house:

"Mr. March, we're sorry to bother you, but somebody did call up headquarters and report that they'd heard a shot here and seen men running away. Do you know anything about this?"

"I certainly do not, sir! Whoever told you that is absolutely crazy! I've been here alone all evening, and there hasn't been a sound! And now, sir. I'll thank you to get out!"

"Do you mind if we search the house and grounds?"

"Well, I certainly *do* mind! What do you think I am, a criminal or something?"

"No, but if we—"

"There is absolutely nothing wrong here, and I refuse to be annoyed by a lot of policemen who don't know what they're doing!"

This was too much for young McGarvey. He stepped forward, waggling a thick forefinger under Elias March's nose.

"Say, if you think you're going to—"

Again Morton grabbed his arm and hauled him away.

"Come on, Garv. If Mr. March says nothing happened, then I guess nothing happened. Let's not bother him any more."

McGarvey crabbed about it all the way down the drive,

but Morton didn't pay any attention to him. Morton was inclined to treat this husky partner of his as a child; and, in fact, young McGarvey wasn't much more than that— except in a fight, when he was worth any three ordinary men.

McGarvey howled, "Say, you can say all you want, but there's something fishy about this business!"

"There's something very fishy indeed about it," Morton agreed, "but we'll never find out what it is by shouting at the top of our lungs. You were probably so busy yelling your head off at him that you didn't notice anything wrong there?"

Now McGarvey worshiped Morton, whom he believed to be the finest detective in the world, but though he tried to imitate Morton, watching him carefully, he never could seem to see the things Morton saw.

"No," he said, crestfallen. "Was there something wrong?"

"There were at least three things wrong. In the first place, March, who was altogether too anxious to get us out, was wearing a heavy flannel bathrobe. On a night as hot as this? There was a light silk dressing robe lying across a chair which would have been a whole lot more comfortable.

"In the second place, that living room was neat as a pin except for the dressing gown—and one other thing. There were no pictures on the walls, but there were at least four places where there had been pictures a little while before. Small pictures, maybe fourteen or sixteen inches long and eight or nine inches high. You could tell that from the fact that those spaces were lighter colored than the rest of the wall. Well, a man might send one picture away somewhere to be reframed or something, but he wouldn't be likely to send four."

McGarvey asked, "What'd that signify?"

"I don't know," admitted Morton. "Maybe nothing at all."

"Well, what was the third thing then?"

"The third thing," said Morton, "is that there was a bullet hole in the wall back of what looked like the dining room door, just above the wood panelling."

McGarvey braked the car.

"Hell! We'll go back there and—"

"No, we won't," said Morton. "I can't be sure it was a bullet hole. It *looked* like one, that's all."

"We'll get a search warrant and find out!"

"I doubt whether we could get a search warrant. That neighbor who called up, whoever it was—the guy at the switchboard didn't get his name, but even supposing we could find him, do you think he's likely to take the chance of getting into trouble with a rich old crank like Elias March? But even if we do get a search warrant, and even if we do find a slug in that wall, where are we? A man like Elias March isn't going to crack open and talk. He says nothing went on there tonight, and he'd stick by his story.

"No, that's out. Absolutely out. But what we do is this: You drop me off here and I'll watch the driveway, and you go on to the nearest phone and get hold of the chief operator and find out whether March has made any calls in the last few minutes—or whether he makes any in the next few minutes. They ought to have a record. The phone was right there in the living room, and it isn't a dial phone, so they ought to have a record."

FIFTEEN MINUTES LATER McGarvey drove back to where his partner loitered, grave and silent, opposite the March house.

"He made a call at 11:13, which must have been right after we left him! He called Dr. Amos Waterhouse!"

"That's what I thought," said Morton, "because Waterhouse drove in there a few minutes ago."

"That guy must have a chunk of lead in him!"

"Maybe. Or maybe it grazed his skin and smashed into that wall. He couldn't have been hurt badly. But maybe he was bleeding. It certainly was a funny thing, wearing that heavy bathrobe on a night like this, when he might have been wearing the silk robe. But I guess the robe had a hole in it that he didn't want us to see, huh? Take that car around the corner."

The physician came out half an hour later. McGarvey, indignant, was all for tailing him home, confronting him, demanding an explanation. But Morton shook a weary head.

"You'll never get anywhere acting that way, Garv. I don't know how many times I've got to tell you that. That stuff may be all right with street corner sports, but not when you're dealing with a rich man like Elias March or a reputable doctor like Waterhouse. If Waterhouse did treat a gunshot wound just now, and if he doesn't report it, then he certainly isn't going to risk his professional standing by admitting the fact afterwards."

"Well, what the hell *are* we going to do about it then?"

"Nothing, probably. Let's go back to the office."

There McGarvey raved on, while Morton, characteristically, went to work at his desk.

McGarvey grumbled, "We go along here all summer, practically dying on our feet for lack of something to do—"

"I've been pretty busy, myself," Morton said.

"—and now when the season's starting up again, and there's a possibility that we might get a little action for a change, and along comes a shooting case, what do you do about it? Nothing!"

Morton, without looking up, waved an impatient hand, like a man who brushes away flies.

"I wish," Morton sighed, "you'd get a nice juicy murder case right about now, to keep you quiet."

"Swell chance! Swell chance of there being any—"

The telephone rang and Morton, who was expecting a long distance call, lifted the receiver and said, "Yes?" He listened for only a moment, and when he pronged the receiver he was almost grinning.

"That's calling your shots," he muttered, half to himself.

McGarvey asked, "What?"

Morton rose, put on his hat. Summer and winter he wore a light-weight, floppety Panama.

"A guy just got murdered over at the Espanola. Come on."

2

CROOKS ROUND-UP

THERE WAS NO reason to connect the two cases. Indeed, as Captain Montgomery remarked gloomily, there was no reason in the world why anybody should take the trouble to kill anybody who looked like *that*.

That was the corpse. It was still warm, and sprawled in the center of a small hotel room, with two blue-black holes in the side of its white shirt. It was the corpse of a man about fifty years old, a squat, appallingly ugly little man with dark hair, tiny dark eyes, a broad and large-pored reddish-purple nose, a mouth virtually without lips. This mouth was pulled open wide, and it was so long that it seemed almost to cut the head in half. It was a weak mouth; but underneath it was a preposterous, pointed, undershot jaw, which gave the whole face the curious appearance of an effeminate, badly spoiled bulldog. The body was little and misshapen, gnome-like, twisted.

A finger-print man was dusting the doorknobs, the telephone, the window sills, the desk; another, using black powder, was messing up the bathroom; and still another was rolling prints from the corpse, working fast in order to get this job done before the fingers stiffened in *rigor mortis*. A camera man had boomed several shots, and the small room still smelled of flashlight powder. Morton, when the fingerprint man was finished with it, went to the one article of baggage, a suitcase.

Montgomery was worried. He was the head of the detective bureau, with the rank of captain, and he was a reasonably good cop; but in matters like this he invariably appealed to his subordinate, Sergeant Wentworth L. Morton. It was an open secret that Morton was the real brains of the bureau.

"Let's have that elevator boy," Montgomery suggested. "He appears to be the only one who can tell us anything— if he's able to talk yet."

The elevator boy was not a boy, but a man. He was as pale as death, and looked a trifle silly with a big white emergency bandage on his head. An ambulance surgeon was at his elbow.

"Now you've got to make this short," the ambulance surgeon snapped. "This man's had a concussion, and he ought to be at the hospital this minute. I oughtn't to let you talk to him at all."

Montgomery said, "All right." He glanced at Morton, but Morton still was busy with the suitcase.

"Who hit you?" Montgomery asked.

"I don't know. There was three guys. I didn't take 'em up, and I'd never seen 'em before. I was just passing this floor when they gave me a buzz and I stopped, and they got in."

"Had you heard the shots then?"

"No, I didn't hear them at all. But when I opened the door for these guys I saw people sticking their heads out of their rooms and asking all sorts of questions, and I was going to stop and see what was happening. It was a cinch *something* was wrong. But one of these guys said: 'Gwan! Gwan down, buddy! We ain't got all night!' They was all in the car then, and behind me. They said to take 'em to the sidewalk level, which is a floor below where the lobby is—"

"We know that. What happened then?"

"Boss, I don't *know* what happened then! The next thing I knew I was laying on the floor of the cage, and it was down at the sidewalk level, and the doc here was swabbing my head with some stuff that stank like hell. I guess one of the guys must have slugged me with something. They was all behind me."

"Would you know any of these men if you saw them again?"

"I might, but I don't think so. They all had their hats pulled down, and they kept their heads low."

"Young fellows?"

"Kind of young, but not kids."

"They look local?"

"No. They had winter clothes on—vests and felt hats and all."

The ambulance surgeon fumed, "Now this man's got to go away!"

"All right," Montgomery said wearily. "Take him away."

MONTGOMERY LOOKED AT Morton. Morton put some letters and papers on the table.

"Looks like his name was Arthur Faurot," Morton said, "and he had some kind of art business in Fifth Avenue, New York."

"Art business?"

"That's what it looks like. Antiques and things like that. We'll wire the print classifications to New York and to

Washington, too. Maybe the customs people know something about him."

Young McGarvey had been uncommonly quiet, for him; but now he confronted Montgomery with a demand:

"This was out-of-towners did this. No three guys from Miami are going to be wearing vests and felt hats. We got to put out a dragnet."

Captain Montgomery had been thinking of the same thing. But he looked toward Morton.

"I don't like that dragnet stuff," Morton said.

Montgomery said, "It certainly wouldn't do any harm. I was thinking only the other day we ought to get busy and have a general round-up here before the season begins."

But Morton said, "I don't care much for that rough stuff. It's too late to pick up many guys tonight anyway. Let's at least wait until we find out more about this guy Faurot."

"But by tomorrow noon—"

"If I haven't got a good lead by tomorrow noon," Morton said, "then all right."

3

MORTON DOES THE BRAIN WORK

McGARVEY CAME ON duty at seven thirty the next day. The office was heavy with rank cigar smoke, and a dusty heap of butts rose above the lip of Morton's ashtray. McGarvey, who didn't smoke, made a face. He started to fan the air with a newspaper.

"Smells like an alligator farm! Don't you ever sleep?"

"I got about an hour's snooze, a little while ago." Morton reached for a carton of coffee, found it lukewarm, stared at the stuff resentfully, wrinkled his nose, and finally drank a little anyway. "I've been finding out about this man Faurot."

"Who was he?"

"He was an art dealer, all right, but I guess he was pretty crooked. He'd been indicted twice for obtaining money under false pretenses in New York, but he beat the rap both times. It was something about phony antiques. Then he was indicted once for possession of stolen property—which was oil paintings—but he had some kind of pull, I guess. Anyway, the indictment was *nolle prossed.* Washington had quite a bit on him, as I'd suspected. He spent eight months in Atlanta once for using the mails to defraud. The treasury people were after him for years because they think he was mixed up with some smuggling outfit."

"Sounds like a bad egg."

"He was high society stuff. When he got in trouble all he had to do was threaten to tell a few things about some millionaire art collectors that he knew—and somebody would work a little anonymous pull to spring him. I guess he really did know a lot about art, from what I hear, but he was a born crook. I can't find out why he came here."

"Maybe he's just on a vacation?"

"There's sport clothes in his apartment in New York—which I had searched while you were sleeping—but all he had with him was a couple of changes of shirts and underwear and socks. That doesn't look like a vacation, does it?"

"You certainly didn't learn all this by Western Union?"

Morton nodded to the telephone.

"Long distance," he explained. "The city's going to have one sweet bill!"

"I think the ole dragnet would be cheaper."

"You never really are happy, Garv, unless you're slapping a flock of punks around." Morton rose, sighing. His muscles were stiff. "Well, when Monty comes, tell him the dragnet's okay by me. It can't do any harm anyway."

"*Hot* dawg!" The rookie bounded out like a jungle ape; but in a moment he was back, while Morton was putting on his hat. "Say, I just happened to think. Do you suppose there's any connection between this guy Faurot being an art collector and the fact that there were four pictures missing from March's house last night?"

Morton, looking at him, almost smiled.

"Oh, you just happened to think that, did you?" said Morton.

He plodded out to get breakfast.

Massive McGarvey, frowning, puzzled, stared after him.

"I wish," young McGarvey muttered to himself, "I wish I knew what the hell Mort's thinking about sometimes."

EARLY IN THE afternoon an old friend of Morton's arrived. Kavanaugh, a member of the New York Commissioner's confidential squad, came down every year to look things over. He was well liked in Miami, and usually there were half a dozen cops there to meet him at the station; but this day there was only Morton.

"You picked a swell time. The rest of the boys are all busy."

Kavanaugh nodded. He was a thin, red-faced man with genial blue eyes. He had hands like a woman and wore his clothes beautifully.

"I know. I read about it in a paper I got when we stopped at Jacksonville. Running out the ole dragnet, are you?"

Morton said, "We got a swell collection of lice up there."

"Shall I look 'em over?"

"Let's have a drink first," suggested Morton.

They had two drinks, and Kavanaugh checked in at his hotel, and they had another drink, and then they went to headquarters. Prisoners and not-quite-prisoners were everywhere—in the cells, in the corridors, at the booking desk, in offices. Kavanaugh, who'd been a New York cop since he was eighteen, knew about every fourth one.

Most of the prisoners, being no account, underworld danglers, and frightened, were willing to talk. Morton spent two hours skimming through these reports, but he found only one item which interested him.

When Kavanaugh had finished looking them over, Morton asked:

"Do you remember a man named George Wilson?"

"Yes. He likes those initials, G.W. He's been George Watterson, and Gerald Whitehouse, and Garrett Welsh and several others. Yes, you've got him in one of the cells up there. As far as I know he's not wanted for anything. He once tried to go big-time and slice himself a little racket cake, but some boys who really are tough waved a chunk of hardware under his nose and said no-no, and he scampered for cover."

"Would he be likely to know Spider Lewis if he saw him?"

"He should. He comes from that same section of Brooklyn."

"And a dope named Reindeers Donnelly?"

"If he knew Spider he'd certainly know Reindeers. They always travel together—though Spider himself never touches the stuff."

Morton said, "This guy Wilson, or Whitehouse, or whatever his real name is—"

"I think the real name is Weissman."

"—whatever it is, he says he's been in Miami three days now and has a job as a bouncer in one of the night clubs out at the Beach, and has not been engaged in any unlawful occupation nor does he intend to engage in any such occupation while here, and that two days ago he saw Spider Lewis and this Reindeers Donnelly in a car in Brickell Avenue."

"Hm-m— Spider Lewis, as far as I know, is not wanted for anything, but he's on parole from Sing Sing—just got out a week or so ago—and unless he's got permission from the Parole Board he has no right to be out of New York State. Did *you* want him?"

"No, except I might like to ask him a few questions. I hear he's a pretty bad boy?"

"Yes," said Kavanaugh, "Spider is not any credit to his parents. He likes to sock people on the head with gas pipes, and shoot people with guns, and things like that. Reindeers Donnelly, I don't know so well, but he's tiny and a coke sniffer, and he has the reputation of being as reliable as a rattlesnake."

"Maybe it'd be a good idea," said Morton, "if we had another little talk with this fellow Weissman."

4

MORTON TURNS BURGLAR

THE MAN TALKED a blue streak, but he didn't really say much. He knew Lewis and he knew Donnelly, and he was sure he'd seen them in a car with two other men in Brickell Avenue two days previous.

"Which way were they going?"

"South."

"What kind of a car?"

"It was a big touring car, dark green. I'd say it was probably a Packard or a Caddy."

"Notice the plates?"

"No, Chief, I didn't. The only thing I did notice was that there was a front plate, so it couldn't be a Florida."

Morton asked Kavanaugh:

"Think New York Identification could have extra pictures of this guy Lewis and this guy Donnelly they could airmail us here?"

"Sure. Send 'em a wire."

"I'll do that," said Morton. He called McGarvey. "You get busy and make out a broadcast describing a car and two guys the way Kav here tells you. Say there'll be a fuller description in a few hours."

Then Morton went for a long walk. He liked walking. It

helped him to think. From time to time he would stop in a telephone booth and call headquarters to learn if there was anything new. The Faurot murder, coming as it did at the commencement of what promised to be a record season, had caused a mighty stir in local political circles, and most of the detectives were working overtime. Morton, strolling, didn't seem to be working at all.

Morton didn't look like a man of impulse; and he wasn't. About most matters he proceeded methodically, carefully, deliberately. Yet sometimes he obeyed hunches, and some of the hunches were pretty strange. He would never admit this to young McGarvey, for he liked the kid and took a paternal interest in him. He'd known young McGarvey's father, and had worked with him for many years. And he was especially staid and cautious in the son's presence, to offset the other's recklessness and keep him out of trouble.

This night he obeyed an impulse, one of those crazy hunches. He found himself far out on Bayshore Drive, in front of the entrance of the March estate, and he decided to do a little burglarizing.

He knew better. He tried to justify himself in his own mind. He told himself that this case apparently wasn't going to get itself solved by ordinary police methods, in which he usually had great faith. He told himself that something special, something extra-legal, was called for.

It couldn't have been just a craving for excitement, the sort of thing that might prompt McGarvey. Wentworth L. Morton was too old, too dignified, for that.

It was close to midnight when he slipped around one end of the hibiscus hedge which lined the front of the estate. The house was touched only here and there by moonbeams, which slipped past a barrier of leaves and palm fronds. It was not large, only two stories high, buff-colored, finished in stucco, a typical Mediterranean style house of the sort common along the east coast of Florida. It was not pretentious, but the grounds were large and well-kept.

Morton went all round it, moving very carefully, now and then stopping to examine a window. He still resembled a bishop, with his square, gray head, his thoughtful gray eyes, even while he was sneaking around like a burglar.

There was no light anywhere in the house, and Morton didn't hear a sound. Fortunately, Elias March did not keep a dog.

The garage doors were open and the garage was empty. It was odd, Morton thought, that Elias March, who was in his seventies, would be out as late as this.

He selected a dining room window, only about four feet from the ground and well shadowed by oleanders. With a jackknife, making never a sound, he cut two small slits in the lower part of the copper screen. He reached a forefinger into each of these slits and threw the latches inside. He swung the screen.

The window itself was locked, but this lock didn't offer much more resistance. The same jackknife blade did the work. It made a slight click. Morton waited for a full minute, heard no other sound. He opened the window and crawled in.

He was, as he had expected, in the dining room. He had no flashlight with him, but he had a full pad of matches.

He went first to the kitchen, where he unlocked the back door and left it ajar. Then he went back to the dining room.

Using matches, and moving quickly along the walls of

the dining room and the library, and the walls of a hall connecting these two rooms, he found no pictures at all, but a total of sixteen places where pictures had recently been hung. The pictures all seemed to have been the same size and shape, as he could see from the rectangles of plaster which were lighter in color than the plaster elsewhere.

He went into the living room, where he knew there were four more such pale rectangles, and there, still using the same jackknife blade, he started to work on the hole above the panelling.

IT TOOK HIM longer than he had anticipated. He spit on the burned matches as he finished them, and dropped them into a coat pocket. He was down to his next-to-the-last one when finally he prised out a small shiny chunk of lead.

He put this into another pocket, sighed with relief, and started for the back door.

Then he heard a car come up the drive.

It came fast, and grated to a stop just in front of the garage. A car door slammed. Morton heard footsteps approaching the house.

He miscalculated. He thought that Elias March was making for the side door, but March made for the back door instead.

Morton, when he learned his mistake, doubled back into the dining room. But he was in too much of a hurry. He knocked over a taboret. It made a terrific crash.

"I'm a lousy burglar," Morton muttered, and made for the open window with no further attempt at silence.

He went through that window headfirst. Oh, he could move fast enough when he had to! He landed on hands and knees, scrambled to his feet, dashed for a row of yuccas rising firm and lovely in the moonlight. The yuccas were in bloom, and the flowers were drooping, waxen, the color of ancient ivory. Just beyond them gleamed the waters of Biscayne Bay.

Morton had made for the back to escape because he supposed that March would guess that a fleeing crook would go for the front, for the Drive. But once again he was mistaken. He heard Elias March's voice behind him, high, angry, but perfectly clear.

"Stop or I'll shoot!"

Morton had sometimes shouted that to fugitives. They'd always stopped. And he'd always thought what fools they would have been to keep on running.

Yet Morton kept on running.

A gun boomed behind him—an enormous, hollow sound. It might have been a deep-throated cannon.

It boomed again.

Morton dived through the yuccas. He stumbled over a rock, turned, picked the thing up, and threw it over the retaining wall into the bay. It made a tremendous splash. Morton ran along the wall a short distance, then slipped back through the row of yuccas. He looked over his shoulder as he did so. Elias March, tall and thin, terrible in his wrath, stood on the retaining wall glaring out over the water. In his right fist, held high, was a stupendous old single-action Colt revolver which must have dated back almost to Civil War days. March was waiting grimly for a head to show itself above the surface.

"Nice gentle old codger," Morton thought as he ran silently to the next estate.

Half an hour later—it was a little after one o'clock—he was back in police headquarters.

There had been no complaint of an attempted burglary in Bayshore Drive. The neighbor who had reported hearing a shot the previous night either had not heard the two shots this night or else had decided that it was not worthwhile to report them. And, obviously, Elias March himself didn't have any desire to talk with policemen.

When young McGarvey finished booking the last prisoner and questioning the last suspect, he went back to the office he shared with Morton. He was hot and tired, worn out. He was astounded to find his partner there, bending over a double microscope.

"I thought you'd gone to bed long ago."

"I ought to have," Morton said apologetically, "only I wanted to compare these slugs. The one on this side has got a right twist of about twenty as best as I can figure it. Five lands and five grooves, plenty plain. So if it's from an American gun it must have been a Smith and Wesson. *That* much is sure. And it looks like it was from a .44 revolver."

He leaned back. The shiny brass barrels of the comparison microscope showed his rounded reflection.

"Well, what's this other slug?"

"That's the one I was examining. It has a right twist of about 20, too. And five lands and five grooves."

McGarvey squinted down the microscope. He nodded slowly.

"Uh-huh. As near as I can see," McGarvey said, "they're from the same gun all right. Sure... No question about it, I'd say."

"That's what I think. But I want to get an expert's opinion on it first thing in the morning, just to be sure."

"Where are these things from, anyway?"

"The one on this side," said Morton, "the doctors took out of Arthur Faurot's body at the autopsy this afternoon. The one on the other side is what I dug out of the living room wall of Elias March's house. Only keep your trap shut about that."

"Mort, you've got hold of something!"

"Maybe. But don't ask me to explain it now. Too tired. Now look: Get down here by six o'clock in the morning."

As they went out young McGarvey pointed to the bottom of his partner's coat, on the left side.

"What the hell have you been doing, trying to burn a hole in yourself with a cigar or something?"

Morton looked, pursed his lips as though the hole were a surprise.

"I guess they can reweave that," he said. "They're pretty smart about that stuff nowadays. Now remember what I said about six o'clock."

5

CROOKS' HIDEOUT

AS A MATTER of fact, they didn't get started until after eight. This was because they had to await the arrival of the airmail with rogues' gallery pictures of Amos "Spider" Lewis and his friend Francis X. "Reindeers" Donnelly. The further cooperation of Kavanaugh was denied to them for the present, that personage having been summoned to Fort Lauderdale to question a prisoner.

"Why south?"

"Several reasons," said Morton. "This man Lewis is a big-timer. He isn't like those maggots you and the other boys scooped up. He's a killer. And if he was in town three days ago, when this guy Weissman said he saw him, why was it that the dragnet didn't get him?"

"He could have gone out the Tamiami Trail—or north."

"He could have, but I don't think he did because of what I think he's got with him. He couldn't stand a search of that car, if I'm figuring this thing right. He and Reindeers Donnelly, and probably the other two guys with them, are well-known criminals, and if they drove north or west at this time of the year they'd be almost sure to get stopped somewhere on suspicion. You know how it is at the beginning of the season? Not only us, but Palm Beach and Daytona and Ormond and Jacksonville and all those places—and the resorts on the West Coast, too, Fort Myers and Bradenton, and Sarasota and Tampa and St. Pete—they're all likely to have special borrowed detectives on hand right now, to check up on just such guys."

"I don't get why they couldn't stand a search?"

Morton didn't answer that. Instead he said:

"And besides, when Weissman saw them, if he's telling the truth, they were driving south near the end of Brickell Avenue. And also, assuming that they were at Elias March's house the other night, about the only way they could have escaped without being seen by the radio patrol boys, who were this side of March's house at the time, was by going south through Coconut Grove. Going that way they could have ducked into Coral Gables or they could have kept on down toward the Overseas Highway. But we notified Coral Gables right away, and if they'd gone there some cop probably would have picked them up, huh? So what with one thing and another, I figure they probably went south."

Now to the south of Miami, which is pretty far south itself, there are only a few small communities—Homestead, Florida City—and then the Keys.

The Keys are hot and almost bare. They support a few gas stations, some stunted, struggling coconut trees, and a multitude of scrub palmettos parched almost brown by the sun.

No other road leads into the Overseas Highway. There is no room for one. Here and there a couple of wheelruts go a short distance to some fishing camp—the region is famous for its fishing—but there is nothing else. Once you are on the Overseas Highway you are, to all intents and purposes, on one long bridge.

There is a single break. A ferry chugs the long trip once a day from Upper Matecombe to Noname Key.

Morton and McGarvey stopped at every service station and showed pictures and asked questions. It was a long, hot, tiresome task. But just south of Florida City, which for all its name is a very small town, they found a man who said "yes."

"Sure, they stopped here a couple of times. The last time was the day before yesterday. Sixteen gallons, and a whole new crankcase full of oil. Paid me with a fifty-dollar bill. That's how I remember it. I had to go all over the place to get change."

"Which way did they go?"

"South."

"Could they have caught the ferry?"

"No, it was too late, no matter how fast they drove. I guess they must've been going to one of those fishing camps."

"Do you remember what kind of plates this Caddy had on?"

"Sure. New York plates. I remember asking them if they knew a friend of mine that used to live in the Bronx. But they didn't."

At Upper Matecombe, which is only a ferry slip, a refreshment establishment and a group of not animated fish guides, nobody remembered having seen a dark green Cadillac, and nobody could identify the pictures. Morton and McGarvey, to make certain, waited for the ferry to return and questioned its crew—with the same result.

Now it was getting dark.

"We'll try all fishing lodges on the way back," Morton decreed.

"We'll get home by about Thursday if we do."

"Oh, there aren't so many."

Young McGarvey, himself an enthusiastic deep-sea fisher, knew all the places, or knew of them. It was a long, slow, wearisome job. But Morton pointed out that the men must be along this highway somewhere—there was no other place they could have gone.

"Maybe they hired a boat somewhere?"

"Then," asked Morton, "what did they do with that car?"

Night brought cooler air, but it also brought mosquitoes. They plugged along, trying one place after another. They were on Key Largo, getting back near the mainland again, when Morton asked:

"Isn't Majorca Lodge along here somewheres?"

McGarvey was tired, disgusted.

"They wouldn't be there. That place hasn't been occupied for six years. It must have fallen to pieces by this time."

"All the more reason to try it. Stop the car a little ways from the entrance and snap the lights out, and we'll walk there."

"They won't be in that dump."

"Well, stop the car, anyway, and we'll see."

One in each sandy wheelrut, walking carefully, they pursued the road which led to Majorca Lodge. There were pines and palmettos on either side—and rattlesnakes too, probably. The pines were not straight and rugged, as in northern climes, but stunted trees which seemed strangely out of place in this hot, forgotten place. Even so, they tried to arch overhead, roofing the road, so that the moonlight was shattered and splintered by their needles. The palmettos clattered fretfully in a wan, half-hearted breeze.

"Waste of time," young McGarvey muttered. Nevertheless he loosened his gun in its holster.

They came upon Majorca Lodge rather suddenly. It was a long two-story structure, originally very grand, designed for Wall Street men who couldn't spare more than a few days, but who were willing to spend hundreds of dollars to get a coat of tan and catch a barracuda, thousands to catch a swordfish or a marlin. That sort of man had abruptly ceased to exist, just as the finishing touches were being put on this lodge; and the company which built the lodge had ceased to exist at the same time; so that none but workmen and servants ever had occupied it, and those only briefly.

AT FIRST GLANCE, with the moonlight full upon it, and the gloriously silvered ocean gleaming beyond a row of coconut palms, it seemed splendid. But presently Morton and McGarvey saw that the white paint had faded and peeled from its walls; the Spanish tiles, once bright red, had been burned a dull pink, and they were falling off. All the windows were smashed; rank weeds and grasses stood brash upon what had been designed as an imposing lawn. Once there had been a parti-colored awning spread over the terrace upon gilded spears. Two of these spears remained upright, but the gilt had long since been scorched off them, or washed off by rains. Of the awning only two lank, faded shreds clung still to the tops of these spears.

Not even the coconut palms had retained their pristine gayety. They'd been pushed this way and that by high winds of the past, and even now, though the breeze was pitifully faint, they leaned far down as though bending before a hurricane. Their lower fronds, untended, drooped dead and brown, burnt out, in hanks which swung dismally, ghoulishly in the breeze.

"Dark," said McGarvey. "Didn't I tell you?"

"Some day," said Morton, "I'm going to take you to an oculist."

"Huh?"

"To your left, out a ways," Morton said wearily.

The water near the shore obviously was shoal. There were little upjuttings of coral which the wavelets lapped. Once a dock had been built out about thirty feet, but this structure had suffered from time and weather even worse than had the lodge building. It was now only a few rotten, dull-splintered piers. However, a little beyond this and to the left, fastened by a painter to something under the water, rocked a bright and shiny Matthews cruiser. It was an open cockpit boat of about twenty-six feet, low and lean and very fast—the sort they used to use in prohibition days to run liquor over from Bimini. It was sleek, alert, smart.

McGarvey muttered, "Well, I'll be gol-darned!"

"But the Cadillac isn't here," Morton pointed out. "Let's mosey around front. Just because there isn't any light showing back here doesn't mean there won't be any in the front."

Somebody behind them said, "What the hell are you guys doing here?"

The accent had warned them what to expect. Not a Northerner, but a typical Florida cracker, thin, malarial, deeply sunburned, in faded blue overalls and a faded blue cotton shirt. He was barefooted and bareheaded. But around his waist was a cartridge belt, and in a holster at his right side hung a large revolver. He had his hand on the butt of this revolver.

It was carelessness not to have drawn the gun. The cracker evidently wasn't used to men of fast action.

McGarvey and Morton, turning, stepped aside—one on each side. They moved unhesitatingly and without a sound, as though they'd rehearsed this in advance. Always in fights, they were like this. They disagreed in many matters, but when the scrapping started they worked together perfectly, understanding one another.

The need was for silence. Morton, snicking out his automatic, struck the man's right wrist with its barrel. McGarvey at the same instant swung at the stomach.

The cracker didn't make a sound, not even a grunt. He sat with a thump, paused there for a moment, and then, as though he thought he hadn't gone far enough, he lay down.

Morton said, "Let's tie a few knots."

The overalls were unexpectedly tough, and Morton had to use his jack-knife on them, but they supplied several yards of binding and gagging material. The cracker wasn't wearing any underclothes. They carried him back into the palmettos.

THEY RETURNED TO the wheelruts, stared with more respect at the mouldering lodge, and encircled it carefully. There was light at three of the front windows.

"Let's slip up closer and get a good look."

"Wait a minute. I think I hear a car coming."

A car was coming from the direction of the Overseas Highway. A heavy car. It lurched and thumped ponderously. A minute later it came into sight. There were no lights on it but the moon showed it to be a dark green Cadillac touring car.

It was brought around in front of the lodge, on the water side. The engine was shut off. A man got out, went to the front door, knocked four times and then once. The door was thrown open, and the man went in.

"Okay now," Morton whispered.

They crept forward. When they got within twelve or fifteen feet of the building they dropped to hands and knees and crawled the rest of the way. Hats off, guns in hand, they rose.

Four men were in the room. Two of them they recognized from pictures as Amos "Spider" Lewis and F.X. "Reindeers" Donnelly. The other two, one of them the man who had just arrived, were strangers.

But the *type* wasn't strange. Morton and McGarvey knew the type well. All four of these men were killers; hardbitten, brutal, cold-eyed, ignorant, vicious. They were violent criminals not by force of circumstances, but by instinct. Their hand was against their fellow men. In any time and in any land they would have been outlaws. They were not clever, and not even possessed of a low cunning as are some animals which hunt alone. They were merely bad—and dangerous as all hell.

Reindeers Donnelly, a wax-faced, half-bald little fellow, sat on a soap box. There was always something in motion about him. He jiggled his fingers, tapped his feet, and his eyes went back and forth constantly, and up and down, never meeting the eyes of any other man.

Spider Lewis, thin and firm, a cigarette stuck in one corner of his bloodless mouth, sat in a chair in front of the only other article of furniture, a table. On this table was a large black automatic pistol, four or five water glasses, two whisky bottles, two old-fashioned kerosene lamps. On the floor below it was a sub-machine gun. Next to Spider stood a hulking, glowering brute, a gorilla for intelligence and for strength, but nothing else except a gorilla. The driver, who was pouring himself a drink when Morton and McGarvey cautiously raised their eyes above the window level, was a plump, dapper fellow, somewhat older than the others, perhaps in his thirties. He wore a purple silk shirt which must have cost fifteen dollars, and a heavy green silk necktie with a pearl pin. His patent leather shoes glittered madly in the light of the kerosene lamps. But his fingernails were rimmed with black.

This man said, "Didn't see old You-All when I came in. Suppose he's on the job all right?"

"He's okay," said Spider Lewis. "That guy never sleeps. Now tell us how you made out?"

"He said 'Go to hell,'" the man downed his drink, stared stupidly at the empty glass. "That was all he'd say. Just 'Go to hell.' So I guess we got to send to New York after all."

The big man growled, "Hell! I'm all et up with mosquitoes in this damned wilderness already. If we hang around—"

"Shut up," said Spider Lewis.

Yes, the type was familiar, and there was nothing strange or unexpected about the large, bleak, dim room in which these men sat—except the walls.

6

STOLEN GOODS

THE WALLS ONCE had been painted buff, but now they were dark brown, a muddy, irregular brown, stained in many places by rainwater from a leaky roof. Large chunks of plaster had fallen out and lay sprawled on the floor, dusty and neglected. Not attractive walls. Certainly not handsome walls. Yet they were decorated, haphazardly but profusely, with Oriental prints of startling loveliness. Dozens of these, neatly framed, hung wherever somebody had decided to hang them, or wherever a nail would hold in the crumbly plaster. Dozens more were on the floor, leaning against the rotten baseboard.

Not any phony antiques from the resort souvenir shop of a mongrel Cantonese, these prints! They were truly great works of art, delicate and precise, each one a masterpiece, each inestimably valuable. Here in this mean hole they depicted scenes of long ago in lands on the other side of the earth—mandarins in polychromatic robes, geisha girls, sleeping Buddhas, wisps of golden incense rising to the painted, gilded ceiling of a palace, dainty and intricate bridges, slant-eyed people who carried paper parasols and paper lanterns bright with color, extraordinary pagodas which tried to reach the sky, temples clustered about by dwarf trees, gardens packed with loveliness, drenched with beauty.

"Well, I don't care," the gorilla said. "I'm getting et up."

Morton touched his partner's arm, and they backed a safe distance to the shelter of some palmettos. When they got there McGarvey whispered excitedly:

"We'll bust in on them! Just shove open the door and walk in with our gats out. We'll round up the whole gang!"

"Are you going to be a kid all your life? These men aren't any Flagler Street jellybeans! They're not going to fall over backwards when you say 'boo' to them!"

"We could cover them before they had a chance to—"

"No, no, you ape! We're not movie actors. When we meet up with guys like this we go about it the right way. I wouldn't tackle that bunch, just the two of us, even if we had a written guarantee that their guns weren't loaded."

"But if we—"

"Here's what we do," said Morton. "I wait here and make sure that they don't go away. It looks as if they were good for the night, but I'll stick around just the same. If they should blow I can run to the nearest gas station, which is only a few miles away, and telephone to Florida City and Homestead to head them off."

"Um-m... And what do I do?"

"You beat it back to the highway, take the car and start organizing a squad. Get all the Monroe County deputies you can get, and all the Dade County deputies too. Get the Florida City cops. Get 'em all the way from Miami. Get 'em with machine guns and tear gas bombs and everything else you can think of."

McGarvey considered.

"Listen," McGarvey said. "I got longer legs than you, and my wind's better—in case there's any need to run for a telephone. And also, this business of organizing a squad isn't as easy as it sounds. *You* could do it like a breeze. But I don't know the names of hardly any deputies around here, and even if I do raise them do you think they'd take me seriously? Maybe you'd better go," McGarvey finished, "and leave me here."

"It would be better," said Morton, "except for one thing. And that is that I can't trust you to keep your head and not go barging into that gang all by your lonesome. I know you, Garv, just like I knew your old man! And I don't want you to get filled full of lead the way he did, because you haven't got sense enough to know that you can't be a whole police department yourself."

"Suppose I promise I won't bust in?"

"All right. *Will* you promise?"

"All right," McGarvey growled, "I'll promise. Now beat it. I'm going to be eaten up by mosquitoes before you get back anyway, so don't be too long about it!"

MORTON, IN FACT, took his time. He left McGarvey promptly, confident that McGarvey would not break his word, but he encircled the lodge slowly, peering into windows, studying the ground, measuring distances with his eye. No business man, no scientist, could have been more careful. The way Morton figured it, there was going to be a battle here soon—Spider Lewis and his crowd would not be likely to submit easily—and it was up to him, as the man who would organize the attacking force, and who would lead the attack, to be sure of the lay of the land.

Eventually he made his way up one of the wheelruts

toward the highway. He walked quietly but rapidly, head down, thinking about things. All these thoughts scurried away when he heard somebody walking toward him. Nimble as any youth, he dodged into the palmettos.

Elias March was coming. His head was high; his dark blue eyes gleamed wildly beneath white brows; his arms, long and limber, swung at his sides. He was hatless, and his white hair, damp with sweat, hung low over his forehead. He was taking long steps. He seemed to know precisely what he was going to do.

In his eyes, in his whole manner, there was a suggestion of the fanatic, the religious zealot. Morton, who never had seen him with this expression, watched him carefully.

March strode on, past Morton, around a curve, out of sight. There was no hesitancy about his gait.

Morton rose, frowning a little, stroking one cheek with two fingers of his left hand.

He muttered, "If that ape would only... But of course he won't. I'd better go back."

So he went back. All his military plans were laid aside.

March was not in sight. Morton crept around to the front of the lodge, didn't see McGarvey, frowned, crept to the side. There was a window there he had previously spotted as the best for his purposes.

He was wondering what the hell had happened to Garv. His gun at a level with his eyes, taking no chances, he rose until he could see over the sill.

Before that, he had heard voices; and even before he heard the voices he could guess what was going to happen.

He saw Elias March in the middle of the room, the four gunmen at the other end, their arms raised. In March's right hand was that huge, single-action Colt of 1880 vintage. March's finger was firm and white on the trigger.

"You think I'd report to the police! You think I'd let it get into the papers, and then have you go wild and destroy these prints because you'd be afraid to be found with stolen property in your possession!"

March, screaming all this time, was walking sideways to a wall. His left hand rose, feeling along the wall for a picture.

"I'll get the police on you in time enough! I'll get them when I know *these* are safe, you sewer rats! The electric chair's too good for you! You ought to be tortured for hours, for days!"

A SHADOW CAME between Morton and the indignation-stiff figure. That native he and Garv had tied up—naked except for his blue cotton shirt, had entered the building by another door. He had his pistol, and it was raised. He wasn't going to shoot. He was going to hit Elias March on the head with the butt of the pistol.

The four men at the other end of the room could see him. They were tense, pale, ready to go for their own guns. But March couldn't see him.

"Why, I'll kill you with my own hands, you vermin! I'll take these back where they belong, and I'll come here and kill you with my own hands! Why, you filthy rats, you ought—"

The cracker swung with his pistol. And Morton, through the open window, shot him in the right arm.

Morton yelled, *"Down!"*

Startled, March turned, and the great weapon exploded with a roar which made the whole building tremble. The cracker, screaming, fell against him. March toppled to the floor, yelling something about sewer rats.

Reindeers Donnelly and the hulking gorilla who didn't care for art, were the only ones with guts enough to go for their guns. Spider Lewis ran, and so did the man who had driven the car.

Donnelly, without any change of expression, snaked out his gun and started to empty its magazine in the direction of Morton. The window glass tinkled above Morton's head.

Morton shot back twice, and Donnelly was still.

Morton was wondering where the hell McGarvey was. March, on the floor, was yelling:

"Don't hit my prints! Be careful you don't hit my prints!"

The gorilla who had been bothered by mosquitoes, threw himself flat on his face. He raised his head, shoved an automatic out in front of him. He began to shoot.

It must have been, Morton figured afterward, the bottom of the window frame, which was just an inch or two above his head. It must have been flying splinters from that. All he knew at the time was that his face flared suddenly hot, and for a split-second he couldn't see anything. He couldn't see to shoot. And he didn't dare to fire wild, for fear of hitting Elias March.

Dimly, foggily, he was aware that the gorilla was leveling an automatic at him. *This* shot would do the job. *This* shot was going to be a careful one.

Then another terrific burst of gunfire, from Morton's right. The gorilla simply put his gun down, and his chin sank an inch or two to the floor, and he died that way—with his eyes wide open, his mouth open, his gun in his hand but flat against the rotting floor.

Morton, still blinking and shaking his head, scrambled through the window. He didn't know, then, that the gorilla was dead. He kicked the gun out of his hand. He kicked the gun out of Reindeers Donnelly's hand. He raced to a front window.

He almost collided, face to face, with young McGarvey. "Are you hurt, Mort? Did those rats—"

Morton yelled, "Get Lewis and that other skunk! They're making for the cruiser! They'll get away!"

He couldn't run after the men without exposing himself to their fire. They had slapped and slushed through the shallow water, and now they were climbing into the fast Matthews. There was only one thing which might stop them. Morton turned, sprang for the sub-machine gun on the floor beneath the bullet-chipped table. He heard the self-starter whipping out there, out in the cruiser, even while he was picking up the gun.

"They'll get away!"

The thought was agony to him. Morton was a man who liked to do things completely and well.

HE RACED BACK to the window, with the sub-machine gun at his right shoulder.

"Careful, Mort!"

The self-starter still was whipping furiously, out in the boat. There was a spurt of orange-colored light there. A gun boomed.

Morton leaned low upon the window sill and fired a burst. The kick of the stock against his shoulder felt good. He held power now.

Nobody would stand against a machine gun.

Purposely he had fired low. He saw the violated water

leap geyser-like. It fell back. Then there was a long silence. The self-starter was still. There was no sign of the two men in the cruiser. Probably they were lying on the floor of that craft.

McGarvey whispered, "That does it. That's the whole outfit."

Morton cried, "Had enough?"

Again silence.

Morton fired another burst—over the cruiser this time—but not too far over. He waited for the echoes to die.

"Had enough?"

A voice clogged with fear floated back, "Okay, Boss. Okay. It's your party."

Morton cried, "Throw your guns overboard!"

There were two loud splashes.

"Now stand up, and take it slow, and keep reaching... Fine! Now step into the water and wade in here... Take it slow."

They didn't look at all tough as they came splashing back, stumbling on the jagged coral, waist-deep, then knee-deep, then ankle-deep in water, and with their hands high. They didn't look tough, they simply looked foolish. McGarvey, all grin, was waiting for them with handcuffs.

And all this while Elias March, paying not the slightest attention to the bodies on the floor, bounded from picture to picture, lifting them in reverent hands, crowing, exulting.

"They didn't hit a one of them... Not a one!"

7

MURDER FOR ART'S SAKE

MORTON EXPLAINED ABOUT Elias March, after they'd
got back to headquarters in Miami. It was dawn. They'd
booked their prisoners and written their reports, and
Morton was having a drink from a bottle in his desk.
McGarvey, who didn't drink, was watching him with
disapproval.

"This guy March," Morton said, "is just batty on one
subject. The way some guys are nuts on postage stamps or
old coins or writing poetry, only in his case it's Oriental
prints. He'd traveled for years to collect those pictures. They
were worth a fortune. He went broke himself—the depression hit him pretty hard, and he hasn't got two hundred
dollars in the bank right now—but of course he wouldn't
sell a single one of the pictures. That's just the kind of a guy
he is. He didn't even like to have anybody else look at them,
and he never lent them to any museum, which is why the
collection wasn't well known. He kept some of them hung
on his walls, but most of them he kept in a closet and just
brought them out now and then, when he was alone, to
gloat over them."

"Some people are funny," McGarvey admitted.

"He'd had both fire and burglary insurance on them,"

said Morton, but lately he couldn't keep up the payments and the policies lapsed. But the money part of it didn't matter to him anyway. Only the pictures.

"Some millionaire art collector who was bitten with the same bug—we'll probably never know who he was—got hold of this man Arthur Faurot, who was a crook from the word go. The millionaire told him that he'd lay sixty thousand on the line for that collection of Elias March's. He'd seen it, and he wouldn't be happy until he had it. He didn't care how. That part of the business was up to Faurot.

"Well, Faurot knew March wouldn't sell, so he came down here and contacted Spider Lewis and his boy friends. They were living at Majorca Lodge. It looked like a nice place for them to lay low. How they ever found out about it, and how Faurot managed to get in touch with them there, we'll never know. But anyway, Faurot offered them twenty grand, cash money, for those pictures. It was a simple business proposition, and it looked like a cinch for them. They didn't try to do any fancy burglarizing, not being guys like that. They just walked in with all iron drawn and stuck March up. He was frantic when he saw them walking off with his beloved pictures and single-handed, with no weapon, he tried to resist them. One of them let fly at him. Lewis says in his confession that it was his friend Reindeers, who was always pretty quick on the trigger, being a dope. The other guy left alive was at the wheel of the car then, so he wouldn't know.

"Anyway, the bullet slid across March's ribs, tearing the skin open, and smacked into the wall. March sort of fainted for a minute. When he came to, the gunmen were gone— with his pictures. Then the cops came. March had only one thought, and that was for the pictures. He took off his dressing robe and put on a bathrobe, to hide the wound in his side; and because he was afraid the gunmen would destroy the pictures if the theft was reported, he refused to admit that anything had happened. Afterward he got his personal friend Dr. Waterhouse to patch him up, and then he took out his old six-shooter and started looking. It's quite a gun. It made a hell of a big hole through my coat when he let fly at me the other night. A bigger hole than any modern gun would make."

"You ought to be more careful," McGarvey said.

"Well, the guys went to Faurot with the pictures, and it seems he tried to stall them, and tried to offer them only ten grand after he'd positively promised twenty. Naturally they didn't trust him. They were sore as hell. It seems Faurot only had ten grand cash with him. And Reindeers Donnelly—again we've only got Lewis' word for this now—Reindeers lost his temper again and went bang-bang. They took the ten grand out of Faurot's pocket.

"WELL, THERE THEY were left with an art collection and they did not know what to do with it. They had no idea how much those pictures really were worth, but they had sense enough to know that they were valuable. They took them down to their hideaway on Key Largo and held a little conference. Somebody suggested trying to get in touch with some other crooked art dealer in New York, but none of them knew any other art dealer, crooked or straight. So then somebody suggested going back to March and offering to give him the pictures back for ten grand. It was a snatch racket, except they were snatching Oriental prints instead of a human being.

"March would have paid them, but he didn't have the dough. And he knew he couldn't raise the dough. The guy who approached him with the offer was that guy we saw drive the car in. They'd picked him because of the whole sweet quartet he was the only one that didn't have a police record.

"March told them to go to hell, and the guy drove back to the Majorca, not knowing what to do. They figured they were perfectly safe as long as they stayed there, and besides they had a guard outside, that native, who was a fish guide and general bum out of work.

"But March had plenty of guts. He's seventy-three years old, and he drives a 1917 roadster, but damned if he didn't tail that guy with the dirty fingernails all the way back to the Majorca, driving without any lights so's the guy wouldn't see him in his mirror! He walked right in on them, mad as hell, and was going to hold the whole pack up and take his pictures back. But then that guard got out of the ties we'd put on him, barges in and spoils the whole thing."

"What I can't understand," said McGarvey, "is why you make me take all kinds of pledges that I won't go busting into something—and then you bust in yourself, one man against five! If they hadn't thought they were surrounded, and that you were a whole squad of cops instead of just one you'd have been slaughtered!"

Morton shrugged.

"Well," he said. "After all, I couldn't stand there and see an old guy like that get slugged. And you weren't anywheres around. I couldn't *find* you," he cried, suddenly indignant.

"Well, I got there in time to lay out that big rat who was just about to pump lead into you!"

"Yeah, you did, at that," Morton admitted.

"How did I know you were going to come back and start making a noise like as if you were trying to be an army all by yourself? You, that's always telling me to be careful!"

"Well, anyway," Morton said hastily, "we cleaned the thing up nicely. Though I was scared for a minute there that Lewis and the guy with the dirty fingernails were going to get away from us. I still can't understand how it was that the boat didn't start."

"The reason for that," said McGarvey, "is that when you went away I figured out that if some dumb deputy fell over his own feet when you were bringing the squad back, these guys' first thought would be to escape by the speedboat. That must have been what they had it there for, I figured. So I waded out there and took the head off the distributor of the engine, and I was just on my way back when all the shooting started, which was why I was a little late."

Morton had poured himself another drink, and he had been about to toss this off. But now he held it, staring at McGarvey over the rim. McGarvey, tired, but flushed with excitement, a boyish gleam in his eyes, grinned back.

"You know, Garv," Morton said, "your old man was dumb as hell, and you're dumb as hell too, just like him. But every now and then I begin to think that maybe you're not quite as dumb as I thought you were."

He drank his drink, and rose, and jammed on his floppety Panama. Young McGarvey was beaming with pride, for Morton didn't very often say anything nice like that.

"Well, I don't know about you young guys," said Morton wearily, "but personally, I'm going home and get some sleep."

THE BLOOD TRAIL

*Morton and McGarvey Follow the Red Trail
That Leads from a Dead Man on the Tamiami
Trail to the Bad Spirit in the Everglades*

1

MORTON FOLLOWS DEATH

THEY WENT VERY fast, the car swaying from side to side. The dawn was late; the morning was chilly, misty; a dirty, low, disagreeable sky, the color of slate, seemed to be trying to make up its mind whether to hurl gusts of rain upon the earth now, or whether to wait a little while.

Not that there was much earth hereabouts. There was the pavement, wan-gleaming and streaked with black like badly tarnished silver; and there was a certain amount of muck on either side of the pavement's banked-up shoulders; but otherwise there wasn't much but sawgrass and water. You couldn't see the water, except in splotches. The sawgrass hid it. Millions and millions of acres, it stretched north and it stretched south, and it stretched ahead on right and left of the Tamiami Trail—unspeakably desolate, poisonous, inhabited only, where it was inhabited at all, by wandering bands of Seminole huntsmen, the only people who can live in that part of the country.

"This guy will chatter when I get my hands on him!" McGarvey said.

Morton said somberly, "You let me handle him, if the Tampa cops haven't ruined him already. This guy would

When you bring your hands out they're going to be empty. Clear?"

rather take everything we can give than run the risk of making a squeal against a man like Adler."

McGarvey's eyes gleamed.

"You really think he is connected with the Adler mob? Boy! If we could clean them up, after half the Federals in the country have been chasing them five months—"

Morton shrugged, sinking deeper in his seat.

"All I know is what they said over the phone. But we're never going to find out *who* he is, if you keep on driving like this."

Young McGarvey said cheerfully, "Well, there's no traffic." He stepped on the gas a little harder. He hummed as he drove—hummed "My Wild Irish Rose" over and over again, very badly but with spirit. He was happy. This was a holiday, practically; for didn't it promise a big-time case, and maybe a man-hunt? McGarvey, being young and huge, and every inch a cop, loved excitement.

His grizzled, clam-like partner didn't feel that way. Morton conducted criminal cases as though they were business deals. He liked to have things go smoothly, efficiently. If a blow were struck, a shot fired—then something was wrong. And Morton didn't like to have things go wrong.

Morton held the side of the rocking car with his right hand. In his left he gripped a piece of paper on which were typed the numbers and descriptions of recently stolen cars. On longish trips he usually held a list like this, and without seeming to do so he watched cars they passed. He was always working, that man. They said of him that he dreamed of his work when he slept—if he ever did sleep.

FOR SOME TIME there was silence except for the younger detective's humming and the rather more musical sound of the engine. Then McGarvey left his wild Irish rose long enough to remark:

"Certainly is lonesome out this way."

It certainly was. They had not passed a car since they left Miami. They had not even passed a lighted gasoline station or fish guide's hut. And of course there were no side roads. The Tamiami Trail is too serious a piece of engineering to fool around with side roads. Straight and firm, with astounding courage it cuts through the very heart of the Everglades.

"Nothing ever happens out here, I guess."

"Something's going to happen pretty soon if you don't quit trying to do seventy," Morton grumbled. Then he sat up straight. *"Look out!"*

McGarvey, who had seen the thing at the same instant, swung the car left and braked it to a slishing, squealing stop.

He turned to Morton.

"Hey!" he whispered, "I think that was a body!"

"I think it was, too," Morton said. "If it wouldn't be too much to ask, Barney Oldfield, would you please turn around and go back, so that we can maybe find out for certain?"

THEY WERE BOTH right. The thing in the road was the body of a middle-aged, thin, rather short man. He wore a gray seersucker suit, good linen, no hat. His face was extraordinarily pale, his hands were cut in a hundred places, and there was a thick, sticky clot of blood on the left side of his head.

McGarvey, who reached him first, knelt, examined the heart. Then he rose, shrugging.

"Dead?" Morton said.

"Yes, he's dead."

Morton knelt in his turn, and made a much more careful examination.

"Another of these damn' hit-and-runs!"

"No," said Morton.

"Huh?"

"This man is soaking wet. The mist would have made him damp, but it wouldn't have wetted him through to his underclothes, the way he is, unless he'd been lying here for an hour or more. And he's warm. He can't be dead more than a little while. Another thing—he wore glasses. See the red arch on the bridge of his nose here, and the two red marks on the upper part of his cheeks? Well, where are those glasses?"

"I never noticed that," McGarvey admitted.

"This man's been walking through the Everglades, and he didn't know how to do it. He isn't a hunter or a fisherman. Not only because he isn't dressed that way, but because he didn't know how to avoid sawgrass cuts. You know and I know, Garv, and anybody who's ever been out here hunting knows, that the edges of sawgrass won't cut you if you graze them with your hand sliding *down*, but if you pull *up* against them they're like razors. This man pulled up."

"But what the hell would anybody be doing walking around in the Everglades at this hour of the morning, in clothes like that?"

"I don't know. That's what we've got to find out. Look— he's pale as a ghost. Must have lost at least two quarts of blood to make him look that way. But where *is* it? There isn't half a cupful of blood here on the road."

McGarvey murmured, "So we got a murder?"

"Yes, we've got a murder." Morton rose. "Here's the stuff from his pockets. Looks like he was A.T. Henderson of Coral Gables. Beat it back to the nearest telephone and get the Gables. Give 'em a good description. And then get the sheriff."

"What are you going to do?"

"Snoop around."

WHEN HIS PARTNER had disappeared in the direction of Miami, the grave, saintly-looking veteran detective examined the corpse once more, briefly. Then he spent a few minutes examining the surrounding ground and pavement. Finally he plunged into the Everglades.

It is dangerous walking in the Everglades. Dangerous not only because of wildcats, alligators, rattlesnakes and cottonmouth moccasins, but also, and chiefly, because of the pitfalls. In the middle of a dry summer parts of this wilderness are no more than stretches of slick mud; but this was winter, and recent rains had been heavy. Morton was a man of average height—though he always looked small standing beside McGarvey, who was a giant—and the water was seldom below his knees; sometimes it was as high as his waist. Beneath it the footing was treacherous— limestone split into fissures of uncertain widths, and black muck and decayed vegetation. Morton, who knew perfectly well that he might at any moment step into a bed of quick- sand, or into extra large fissure, to disappear forever and without a sound, moved cautiously, placing his feet with elaborate care. He treated the sawgrass with respect, too— the respect of a man who knows how viciously it can cut.

The dawn had come at last, and rather abruptly, as though eager to make up for being late. A warm sun was shining. The mist was low and thinning. The top of the grass was at all times above Morton's head, so that he could not see more than a few feet....

He was following a waterlead. The Everglades are filled with them—some the width of brooks, some like rivers. They are paths among the sawgrass, natural paths, with all the aimlessness of nature. They wind here and there, turn back upon themselves, branch a hundred ways, dead- end. Some of them open into lakes. Some terminate at the stubby little mud islands with which the wilderness is relieved—islands which support a few cabbage palms, a few sun-dried palmettos, perhaps a cypress or two, sometimes even pines, almost invariably a multitude of poisonous snakes.

When the water got above his knees he unstrapped his pistol, which ordinarily he carried at his belt on the left side ready for a belly-draw, and fastened this around his neck. He waded on.

He was following a trail of blood. And as he went he used his handkerchief and the end of his coat to break off-pieces of sawgrass, marking the way. Nothing could be easier than to get lost in this place. The silent Everglades have swallowed uncounted men, and they leave no traces.

The blood trail ended, but the waterlead continued. Morton followed it a little further, hoping to find further droppings of gore. It opened into a lake.

They are called lakes, though they have no banks. They are open spaces, clearings among the sawgrass, that's all. This one was almost perfectly round and perhaps fifty yards across. On Morton's right, twenty feet or so ahead, there was a gentle "ploo-oop," and the water was disturbed for an instant. "Alligator," he thought. There was no other sound, and no movement except for the five buzzards which wheeled tirelessly in wide awkward circles overhead.

Morton sighed a little. He knew that his search was ended for the present. The water in the lakes is usually deeper than in the leads, but even if he had a canoe he would not be likely to find any more drops of blood.

He reached for his pistol, wishing to make sure it still was dry before he started the return journey.

THE RATTLING, RAIN-LIKE sound of lead pellets among

the sawgrass on his left came to him at the same instant as the boom of the shotgun. He stepped backward, bending his knees. The gun boomed again, and the water all around him sprang to life, whitening gloriously. He saw a canoe dart out of the end of a waterlead at the other side of the lake. It was an Indian pirogue, a dugout, with a high stern, on which stood the man with the shotgun; this was why the man had been able to see Morton when Morton couldn't see him.

Morton glimpsed this much. He was bringing down his pistol for a shot at the man in the bow when he stepped into a fissure.

It threw him backward. He never had a chance to catch his balance. He went under with a loud splash.

A moment later, when his head came above the surface, he saw the muzzle of a large black automatic. It wasn't a yard from his face. Three men were in the canoe, one with a pole, one with the shotgun in which he was putting a couple of fresh shells; the third held the automatic.

"All right, buddy. When you bring your hands out they're going to be empty. Clear?"

Morton was quiet about it. He had been in too many tight places to be ruffled. Yet the sight of the speaker sent a surge of excitement even through his case-hardened breast.

He dropped his pistol, under water, and slowly raised his arms.

"What are you doing? *Kneeling* there?"

"Yes, I'm kneeling."

"Well, stand up and climb into this boat."

"I can't. My foot's caught."

"Your foot's caught, huh? Well, we'll pull you out."

The man with the pole was a Seminole, gaudy with a yellow, carnation, nile green and purple jacket and wooden beads. A guide. There was no expression on his fat face. He pushed the canoe a little closer.

The speaker, putting aside his automatic, grinned. He seemed pleased with himself.

"Recognize me, huh?"

Morton did not answer.

"Well, we'll pull you out," the man repeated. He leaned over the side and put his arms under Morton's arms. He was a short man, with stumpy legs, but his body was huge.

Morton warned, "Take it easy."

"Oh, I'll take it easy all right, buddy!"

The man gave a sudden, terrific jerk. Morton's face went white, and beads of sweat pushed away the Everglades water on his forehead. His eyes squeezed shut. But he didn't make a sound.

Stumpy-Legs lifted him bodily into the canoe, dumped him to the bottom. Morton lay motionless, his eyes still shut.

"That must have hurt him," the man with the shotgun suggested.

"He fainted. I guess he can't take it, the louse."

"Let's get out of here."

"Sure we'll get out of here," Stumpy-Legs said. "Sure we will. What the hell do you think?"

2

―

LAKE OF BAD SPIRITS

WHEN HE RETURNED, with two deputy sheriffs trailing him in another car, McGarvey was not at first alarmed to find the body unguarded. He had illimitable confidence in his partner, and he knew Morton's habit of prowling around the scene of a crime to see things other men didn't see—and his habit of keeping those things to himself until he could understand how they fitted together. Morton, as even young McGarvey himself admitted, was the brains of the pair. McGarvey did the driving, the checking; when necessary he did a full share of the fighting, but he was not ordinarily called upon to use his head. And so, being naturally lazy, he didn't.

"Nice way for him to leave a stiff," one of the deputies muttered.

McGarvey flared, "Do you think *you* can tell Sergeant Morton how he ought to run a murder case!"

"All right, all right. Don't get excited."

"I'm not getting excited, but Mort knows more about murders than you and all your family will ever learn!"

"It'd be different," the other deputy said, "if this *was* a murder. But it's nothing but an ordinary hit-and-run."

"It is not! It's a murder!"

"How do you know all that?"

"Because Mort said it was!"

There was something irresistibly small-boyish about McGarvey at moments like this—something his great size only accentuated. One of the deputies snickered a little. McGarvey approached him, eyes blazing.

"All right," the deputy said. "All right, it's murder then!"

"You're damn well right it's murder!"

"But just the same, I can't understand why the sergeant walked away and left the stiff here."

"Mort knows what he's doing," McGarvey grumbled.

Still, McGarvey himself was beginning to get worried. Morton, he knew, might have wandered a short distance, looking for clues, but he would not get beyond earshot of the highway. And McGarvey had made a lot of noise returning to this spot. He had even tooted his horn a few times.

He went to the car and tooted that horn again. He was frowning, half angry, half scared. The deputies were examining the body.

"You better not move that thing," McGarvey warned. "Not until it's been photographed, anyway."

He tooted the horn once again. He kept looking around; but there was nothing east and west except the bare wet highway, gleaming silver now in the warming sun, and nothing north and south but the blank expanse of the Everglades.

After a while he went back to the body, and examined it again. Yes, it was wet clear through to the underclothes, the way Morton had said, and the hands and wrists were red with small ugly cuts. McGarvey inspected the edge of the road, the banked masses of sawgrass. Presently he found a waterlead at the end of which a blade of sawgrass had been broken. And on that blade he found a drop of blood.

The person who shed that blood had been moving out of the Everglades and toward the road. That is, he had been moving in that direction unless the blood came from one of his hands which he was swinging backward at the time—and this was unlikely, in such a place.

"Um," said McGarvey, and started to wade into the water. Somebody behind him called a warning. You never knew what you might step into, in this country. McGarvey paid no attention, and possibly he didn't even hear. He had found another drop of blood, a little further on; and this drop had fallen from somebody wading *into* the Everglades, *away* from the highway.

It was not difficult to see this, now that the sun was out. Drops of blood falling from a person who is moving resemble in form drops of rain falling against a window; they tend to be pear-shaped, and have little tails.

McGarvey found more of these as he went, some pointing due north into the very heart of the Everglades, some pointing back toward the Tamiami Trail.

He followed this waterlead for several hundred yards, until he came to an almost circular lake. He didn't dare go any further. Besides, he had not been able to find any more drops of blood.

THE LAKE WAS deserted. It was more than deserted; except for a few broken blades of sawgrass at the end of the waterlead, where McGarvey stood, there was nothing to indicate that any human being ever had passed this way. The place looked bleak and dead, millions of miles from anywhere. No birds stirred, no animals. The surface of the water was unbroken. Far ahead, to the north, five buzzards wheeled in slow, lumbrous circles. But this meant nothing; there are always buzzards in the Everglades.

McGarvey began to shout. *"Mort! Oh, Mort!"* There was no answer, though he waited a long while. Then he called again, and again he waited; but still there was no answer.

Far ahead the buzzards flew around and around, very low. McGarvey couldn't go to that place without a boat, without a guide as well. Behind him he heard shouts, the blat of an automobile horn. They were getting worried about him.

He turned, panicky. And as he turned he stepped upon something hard under the muck.

The mud and water were about his knees, and he didn't dare to plunge beneath the surface. Carefully, sweating with anxiety all the while, he worked the object against his left leg with his right foot. He raised it a little distance, reached for it. It slipped. He repeated this, and caught the thing a second time. But it cost him his balance. As he was lifting the object above the surface he toppled, stepped into a fissure, fell.

He managed to get up again, but only to his knees. His left foot was caught.

The water, when he was in that position, was almost as high as his chin. He began to yell. But his voice was strangely weak.

The buzzards came nearer, circling low. Perhaps they had heard his cries, or perhaps with carrion instinct they sensed the presence of near-death. For they live upon death, those birds. They feast upon swift putrefication under the hot, wet Florida sun.

It was almost an hour before the men from the road found him. *They* weren't fools to be wading into the Everglades. *They* had gone to the trouble of getting a guide from a Seminole village to the west, and they went as a rescue party in a sound, dry dugout.

By that time the buzzards were very close, wheeling around McGarvey's exposed head, sometimes almost brushing him with their black and rusty-brown wings. They stank horribly; and there was blood on their beaks. McGarvey was roaring curses at them.

"You better get yourself to a doctor, fella. You're in no shape to go on working today."

"Doctor hell!" Young McGarvey stabbed a long arm at the Seminole, who stood impassive in the stern. "You! You're hired, right now! I'm going to need you!"

THEY THOUGHT, WHEN they saw the way he behaved, that McGarvey'd gone off his nut waiting there. But he hadn't. He knew what he was doing. He simply didn't have time to stop and explain.

It had not been easy to figure out, especially for a man who was accustomed to letting another do his thinking for him. A dozen times he had wished, while he shouted curses at those buzzards, that he was possessed of the quick, sure mind of Morton. But just the same he had muddled it over, and had found, somehow, an answer.

"Couple of you guys help me with this canoe. Come on! It goes up on top of my car."

"Say now, take it easy, Garv. You can't go—"

"Take it easy hell!"

"The guy isn't ever going to get any deader than he is."

"Him?" McGarvey waved contemptuously toward the corpse. "I'm not worried about *him!* Do anything you want with *him!*"

"But you got to make out a report."

"I'll do that later!" He shoved the canoe into place, doing a large part of the work himself. He fastened it there by ropes running to the front and rear bumpers. Then he grabbed the Seminole, pushed him into the front seat. "Come on, Charlie!"

He drove west.

But he didn't drive fast. He went very slowly and carefully, watching both sides of the road. Four or five times he stopped, got out, examined the edge of the sawgrass.

About four miles from the place where Henderson's body had been found he came upon a deserted gasoline station. It was a miserable shack, once white but scorched by the sun and washed by heavy rains until it had become a sickly, uncertain gray. It was on the north side of the Trail, and apparently was built upon a foundation of cypress which had grown rotten. The whole building sagged badly, and the single gasoline pump in front of it, like the building practically colorless, also sagged. Weeds crowded it. In the rear there was a drive about ten feet wide. Beyond that the wilderness rose triumphant.

"Nobody occupy this place, Charlie?"

The Seminole, whose name probably wasn't Charlie at all, grunted a negative.

McGarvey peered in a window—the glass was broken. He went behind the place. He got down on hands and knees.

After a while he said, "Oh." He studied the wall of sawgrass in the rear. An exceptionally wide waterlead ended there. It was fully eight feet across, but so sinuous that very little of it was visible. Some of the sawgrass at its edges was broken.

McGarvey hurried back to the Seminole.

"There's islands back there, Charlie?"

Charlie shrugged.

"I asked you if there were islands back there!" McGarvey said again.

"Some islands," the Indian admitted.

"All right then. You're going to take me to 'em. Get this canoe off the top."

They launched the pirogue. McGarvey, furiously busy, tossed his companion the pole, grabbed a bow paddle for himself, scrambled in.

"Come on."

The Seminole said, "No."

McGarvey got out of the canoe, moving very slowly. He came close to the Seminole.

Both men were big. There was no expression on the Seminole's face, but he held himself stiff with the pride of his tribe, the only unconquered Indians in the United States. McGarvey got very close to him.

"Let's get this straight, Charlie. I said you're going back there with me, and you're going to pole, and you're going to show me those islands."

The Seminole said, "No."

McGARVEY, WHO WAS a powerful man, hit him smack on the chin. The Seminole staggered, scowled, raised his hands—and McGarvey hit him again. The Seminole went down.

McGarvey sat on his chest and drew a pistol. McGarvey's face was purple-red, and not pleasant; his eyes were blue ice. He waved the pistol under the Seminole's nose.

"Now listen. I'm in no mood for fooling around. Are you coming with me, or am I going to put a slug into your mouth?"

The Seminole said, "No."

It was puzzling. These Indians of the Everglades, as McGarvey knew, are no cowards. And they're stubborn. But there was more than mere stubbornness acting here.

McGarvey asked in a quieter voice, "Just what is it you've got against this place?"

The Seminole rolled his eyes toward the sawgrass.

"Bad spirit there."

"I think so too, but not the kind you're talking about."

"Bad spirit. My friend go there many weeks ago, hunting alligator. He not come back. Bad spirit take him."

"Maybe it was only a rattler, or a moccasin?"

"No. Bad spirit."

McGarvey said "Um," and rose, staring at the sawgrass. The Seminole did not stir. McGarvey looked down at him, looked over his left shoulder at a slip of purple pasteboard which had been dislodged from the weeds by the Indian's fall. McGarvey picked it up.

A pad of matches, about half filled, bearing the advertisement of the Crescent Flats Hotel, Memphis, Tenn.

McGarvey said "Um" again, and asked the Seminole, "Is this friend of yours a good guide? Know his way around in these parts?"

"He best guide in Florida."

"And it was how long ago that he disappeared?"

"Six-seven weeks ago."

McGarvey stared for a long time at the sawgrass, all the while gently joggling the pistol he still held in his right hand; the pad of matches was in his left hand.

"So that's the way it is," he whispered.

3

PUBLIC ENEMY NO. 1

WHEN MORTON RECOVERED consciousness he was lying in mud between two automobiles. They were not very pretty cars. They had no tires, no batteries, no accessories of any sort. For that matter, they didn't even have seat cushions. There were, nearby, two similarly stripped cars.

"So you recognized me, huh?" said the man standing above him.

Morton moved his eyes. His head ached a little. His left ankle hurt furiously, but otherwise he seemed to feel all right.

"I ought to recognize you. Your picture's been in the papers enough times lately."

Stumpy-Legs, who was George ("Nutsy") Adler, Public Enemy Number One, grinned amiably.

"Yeah, they got a lot of pictures of me," he admitted. "But what surprises me is that you're willing to admit it."

Morton sighed and closed his eyes.

"Why not?" he murmured. "You wouldn't believe me if I lied to you anyway."

Adler kicked him. Adler was grinning all the time, but there was plenty of force in the kicks, which struck Morton on the right side of the chest.

"Open your eyes when you talk to me, cop."

Morton opened his eyes.

"What do you think of my new racket?"

Morton looked around, nodded at the sight of the cars.

"Pretty small potatoes for a man like you, isn't it?"

Adler grinned the broader. But his eyes, which were long and hard and dark green, showed none of the affability of his mouth.

"Sure it is. But we got to do something to keep busy. We haven't got any dough except dough that's hot and that we don't dare to shove around for a while. We was thinking of busting into your town, cop, and pulling some fast job, but we decided from what we read in the papers that there's too many G-men there right now."

"Yes, the city's thick with them. All this end of the state is. They know they've got you down here somewhere, and they say they're just going to keep on looking until they find you."

"Yeah?" Adler's mouth was drawn back tight now, and he wasn't grinning any longer. "They're never going to find us in *here*, are they?"

"You like it here?"

"No. Too many mosquitoes. But it's got advantages." He looked around. "For one thing, it's a swell place to cool off. And a swell place to get rid of stiffs in."

"You were a little slow with the last one."

Adler frowned.

"We thought that guy was cold. Then when we get him a little ways back, in that canoe, thinking to weight him and sink him, all of a sudden he tumbles out and runs back through the water toward the highway. We couldn't get the damn boat around fast enough. That damn Indian… At that, we could have finished the guy off just after he got to the road, only we heard you coming. You were coming fast, and we figured you'd breeze right on."

"But we didn't."

"Which," said George Nutsy Adler, "was your hard luck."

"I've got a friend."

"You could have a hundred of them, and they wouldn't find you here. Just the same, we're keeping you on ice for a little while."

"I'm a hostage, eh?"

"Is that what they call 'em?"

THERE WAS SOME silence, while Morton, still on his back in the mud, examined this man closely. Without those green eyes trained on you, Morton reflected, the nation's current Public Enemy Number One was anything but impressive. He was ape-like with his huge body and bandy legs. He wore a very dirty shirt of heavy pink silk, no collar or tie, a ragged, dirty Panama hat, dark blue trousers with a gray pencil stripe, black and white sport shoes. Most of the time he held his head back and his chin up, in an arrogant, Napoleon-like fashion; but his voice was generally soft, almost like a Southerner's voice. He was officially known to have killed nine men.

"That damn Indian," he muttered again.

The Seminole had gone off on a raft, with one of the Adler followers. The Seminole was doing all the pole work. The gangster merely watched him.

"Where did you get him?"

"We ran out of gas and we stood a sweet chance of

getting caught. Then along came this baby in his canoe. We made him show us to a place where we'd be safe."

"Those fellows usually keep out of trouble," Morton said.

"This one wanted to." Public Enemy Number One grinned, and again the detective got a cold feeling at the sight of those green eyes. "But the way we put it up to him, he decided different."

"What are you going to do with him?"

Adler still was grinning.

"The same thing we're going to do to you. All in good time, cop, all in good time."

HALF AN HOUR later the raft reappeared, the Indian still poling it. There were two gangsters on it now, and there was also a Ford coupé. Morton thought, A.T. Henderson's car. But he didn't move.

Nutsy Adler walked to the edge of the water.

"Come on," he called to the three on the boat. "I want to get this crate safe here and then go back to the other island. Somebody might come looking for this cop."

There were three gangsters besides Adler, who did no work. They were thin-chested, ratty, silent fellows, covered with pimples and mosquito bites. The Seminole had to do most of the labor. It didn't take long, even so, because there was practically no bank on the shore and they made the raft fast with ropes to long stakes driven into the more solid ground in the center of the little island.

"All right. Now we leave that there, and get back where nobody's going to find us," said Nutsy Adler. He did not address the men by name. This was no precaution against the presence of Morton; it was pure contempt. He simply

called them "you." The Indian he scarcely noticed until he
was ready for the pirogue.

"Get that boat around, you. And make it snappy."

Deliberately, with a muddy foot, he kicked the Indian.
The Indian turned, paused. Adler snicked out an automatic.

For a moment the Indian did not stir. Incalculable
generations of warriors were behind this red-skinned
survivor—but perhaps they were too far behind. Eventually he cowered in the presence of Public Enemy Number
One. He shrugged, turned.

Adler kicked him again. "And make it snappy!" To
Morton he said, "All right. We're leaving for the interior."

Morton rose slowly. The Indian was unpaintering the
pirogue, which was near the raft. Morton saw him work
it clear of the mud, step in, and take the pole. One of the
gangsters yelled, "Hey!"

The Indian had given the boat a tremendous push as he
jumped into it. Now, with the pole, he gave it another push,
and another, and another....

He was making for the cover of the sawgrass.

George "Nutsy" Adler leveled an automatic at him,
started shooting. Adler was perfectly cool about it, and
fast. Morton took a step toward him—but it was all over by
that time. Even while the gun was thundering, the Seminole seemed to leap forward. He fell flat to the bottom of
the canoe, and the pole floated free. He wasn't ducking,
either. He had been hit square in the spine.

"The fool," Nutsy Adler said with feeling. He turned to
one of the gangsters. "Go out there and get that boat back.
And if the sap's still alive, give him a couple more."

But the Indian wasn't alive. And Adler, who had

slaughtered him, blazed in a terrible rage. *He* didn't know anything about this wilderness in which he found himself, and neither did any of his followers. They were utterly lost without the Indian.

The sun, as though at a signal, moved swiftly behind a dark and very low cloud. A chill breeze sprang up, rustling the tops of the sawgrass.

Morton smiled. Adler, snarling, sprang upon him, slapped his left cheek hard with the barrel of the automatic. Morton didn't move after that, and he was careful not to smile again.

Adler put another clip into the automatic.

"I'll find the damn place," he muttered.

One of the men said, "Cripes, Nutsy, if we ever get lost—"

"Shut up! I've done it enough times. I know the way." He swaggered to the boat, climbed in. He went to the bow. "You, cop—you get in the back and work that pole. And you make it go the way I tell you to! The rest of you get in the middle here."

WENTWORTH L. MORTON was fifty-odd, but in fine physical condition. Uncomplaining, he stood in the high stern, so that he could see for a short distance over the top of the sawgrass, and he poled patiently, firmly, as well, possibly, as the Seminole himself could have done the job. He never said a word. Though it was chilly now, sweat shone upon his face from the exertion, and all down his body he could feel sweat making his clothes cling to him.

Sometimes he glanced at the four city rats in front of him, sitting or lying in the native canoe. They looked so ludicrously out of place! They had pistols in their laps, and they stared at the sawgrass as it slid past the sides of the canoe; listening to this deafening silence, they were beginning to know panic.

Even George "Nutsy" Adler was losing his confidence. From the beginning he had been hopelessly lost. But he wouldn't admit this—not for an hour or so. And even after that he sometimes rose in his place, frowned at a branching waterlead, and snarled, "Turn to the right here," or "Swing to the left." Morton invariably obeyed. But in fact Morton was going the way he wished to go.

It was a big half-circle. It had to be big. Once these men suspected him, he was dead. Dead, and his body never found. Food for the alligators like those poor waylaid motorists, and that poor Seminole guide.

So he made the half-circle a big one. While he permitted Adler to believe that the boat was headed north, deeper into the Everglades, he was turning it slowly south. All this country looked the same to the gangsters. For that matter, it all looked much the same to Wentworth L. Morton. But he was not wholly without experience in the Everglades. There were small direction indicators his practiced eye could see. And best of all there was the breeze. The breeze was a wet one, bringing rain. The rain was a mere drizzle at first, but it grew steadily more impressive, harsher; and the breeze itself stiffened until it was definitely a wind.

Storms in this part of Florida, at this time of the year, Morton knew, usually came from the direction of Biscayne Bay. That was due east. So Morton got the wind straight against his left cheek, and figured, and hoped and prayed, that he was poling the boat precisely south. The Tamiami Trail was south.

What he most feared was that they would encounter again that small island, presumably near the Trail, where the Adler gang dismantled their stolen automobiles. They might, indeed, come upon that place at any turn of the waterlead. Standing in the stern, he could sometimes see over the sawgrass, and he kept his gaze sharp for sight of any unusual elevation.

For a long while he saw nothing but the sawgrass itself, stretching in a dull brownish blanket on all sides. This was an aquatic Sahara, it seemed. Nothing but water and grass.

Then he saw something which made him gulp hard—made him almost topple out of the canoe.

What he saw was the head of young McGarvey.

His partner was apparently standing in the stern of another pirogue, using another pole, in another waterlead not more than thirty feet away. Then Morton saw that it *wasn't* another waterlead. It was the same one in which he was traveling! McGarvey was coming toward them! The waterlead was twisty, and McGarvey, his big face red with exertion, had not yet seen Morton's head. But he was coming toward it, just the same.

Morton thought, "Oh, the fool! The big bull-headed, brass-gutted Irish fool! Somehow he's trailed me here, or more likely it's accident. He's going to do everything alone, by himself. He'd charge an army, that kid!"

And encountering the Nutsy Adler mob in this desolate place would be no less dangerous than charging an army, at that.

There they were—four street rats, four desperadoes, each a murderer. Four men with guns, wanted everywhere and knowing, if they knew anything, that sooner or later they would be cornered and mowed down by machine gun bullets—here they were crouching in a canoe. And young McGarvey, in something less than two minutes, would be calling upon them to surrender.

IT WAS SO like young McGarvey! The best kid in the world, the loyalest sidekick any cop ever had—but a dumbbell just the same. A dumbbell who never asked the odds against him, and never cared.

Morton brought the pole forward for another grip. He pushed it in deep. He pushed himself right over backward.

As he fell he screamed, *"Down, Garv! Down!"*

Water carries sound. To Morton, down among the sawgrass roots, down in the thick Florida goo, it was as though the whole world had exploded. It almost burst his eardrums. It bellowed deep and terrible, not like mere pistol fire but like the great roar of coast defense guns.

When he came to the surface it wasn't half as bad as that. It sounded, then, like a mere pip-pip-pip though there was a lot of it. It sounded like a series of tiny firecrackers all strung on one fuse-string, clittering away furiously while the echoes of a giant cracker still hang in the hot Independence Day air.

A gangster was draped over the side of the pirogue, his head and arms in the water. Another was forward, his arms raised, screaming for mercy. One was floundering through the water behind Morton somewhere. But George "Nutsy" Adler was erect, and his gun arm was straight. His big automatic was bobbing in his hand as he fired. Morton caught a glimpse of young McGarvey, a smoking revolver in his fist, wading noisily through water waist-deep. Adler saw him at the same instant, and leveled the automatic at him.

Morton reached over the side of the pirogue and grabbed Adler's legs. And they both went under water.

When Morton came up his partner was slapping his shoulders.

"You all right, Mort? Did those thugs hurt you?"

"Down that way, gorilla," Morton pointed. "There's one of them wading away."

"That's all right, the other boys'll get him," McGarvey soothed.

"The other boys? You mean to tell me you had sense enough, for once in your life, to bring help with you?"

"Sure. I brought four deputies. That was all I could get together right off the bat. I had them lying in the bottom of the canoe. I was going to do all the poling myself, so's I'd draw off the Adler gang's fire if they saw me before I saw them."

"And you even knew what gang it was you were coming after?"

"Are you hurt at all, Mort? What's the matter? Why don't you stand all the way up? What you got underneath the water there?"

"This," Morton tugged at something, "is a Public Enemy Number One, in first class condition, except maybe a little wet."

"Bring him up. I've always wanted to clout a Public Enemy Number One."

"Don't hurry me!" Morton said. "I'll bring him up in a minute. Think of all the fun I'm having doing this."

4

McGARVEY GROWS BRAINS

MORTON WAS QUIET about it, afterward. He didn't read McGarvey one of his little lectures. He was too old and too wise openly to praise his partner, but he grunted some commendation—which was a lot from old Morton.

McGarvey was elated at this bit of praise. He told Mort:

"The first thing I figured, after I got out to that lake and happened to find your gun—that was just a break, of course, just dumb luck—well, the first thing I figured was that this must be some alligator hunters going gaa-gaa and holding up motorists. But then I thought: How could they get rid of the cars? I'd learned over the telephone from Coral Gables that this guy Henderson had a car, a Ford coupé, and that he had started for Tampa in it early this morning, just a little while before we started. Well, where had it gone? If it had been driven toward Miami we would have seen it ourselves. So it must have gone the other way. They wouldn't take the chance of driving all the way to the west coast in a car as hot as that, and there aren't any side roads, so I figured they must have taken the thing on a raft or something back to one of the islands. So I went looking for a place they could have done that from.

"Then when I found the place I couldn't persuade my

Indian guide to take a chance on poling me back there. He was scared of a bad spirit he said had taken his friend six-seven weeks ago, in that district. It was just six-seven weeks ago that the federals figured Nutsy Adler and his gang got down into this part of the state somewhere. And where would be a better place to hide than in the Everglades—provided they could find a guide? Alligator hunters wouldn't need a guide, but city gangsters would.

"It made it that much more certain when I found on the ground there a pad of matches from the Crescent Flats Hotel in Memphis. That was the hotel the G-men raided, about eight weeks ago, looking for Adler and his gang. They were four hours too late."

"It probably isn't a big hotel," Morton said quietly, "but even so, somebody else might have dropped such a pad of matches."

"Yes, but whoever used these matches was left-handed, and Nutsy Adler is left-handed, which made it practically certain."

"How did you know that whoever used the matches was left-handed?"

"They were about half used up, and they were pulled out from the left side. A right-handed man would hold them in his left hand and pull them out with his right—from the right side. Okay?"

Morton looked at him for a long moment. They were back on the Tamiami Trail now, putting two prisoners into a police car—the other two gangsters were to travel horizontally, one in an ambulance, one in the morgue wagon.

"You know, kid," Morton growled, "if you don't stop getting brighter and brighter you'll turn out to be a detective yet some day. Come on." He got into their car. "We still have to go talk with that punk the Tampa cops are holding. We're four hours late now."

"Well, the way I figure is, Mort, I figure this Henderson murder was a case that called for immediate action."

"Yeah. Well, the Tampa pick-up isn't. So don't try to make seventy in this crate again, will you? It's all right for you kids, but I'm getting too old for excitement like that."

FOOLS CAN BE DANGEROUS

*The Mystery of the Strangled Millionaire, the
Murdered Greek, and the Strange Black Box*

.

1

STRANGE CARGO

THE WHOLE BUSINESS started as an incident of ordinary police routine. Nobody dreamed, when Morton and McGarvey were ordered to "de-punk" the city, that they were going to turn over one of the biggest murder cases in its history.

Miami gets some wonderful visitors in winter. It also gets others not so wonderful. Indisputably, wherever so many millionaires are gathered together for holiday purposes there's a flock of dips and confidence men, jewel thieves, gigolos, phony security salesmen, burglars, gamblers, and just common ordinary bums. The police sometimes get rid of these personages, when there is no legal justification for an arrest, by the simple process of kicking them in the pants and telling them to get the hell out. It's not original, but it works.

"You'll either tell us who's in town or else I'll take you to pieces!" McGarvey slapped the prisoner's head with two open hands. "Cough it up, louse!"

They had nothing against this particular man—a mere pick-up, a safecracker Morton had recognized in the street. They had found no gun on him, no burglar's tools, no stolen goods. But before they put him on a northbound train and sent wires to the police of West Palm Beach and Jacksonville to make sure that he *stayed* on that train, they wished to get from him whatever information he might have concerning his fellow undesirables.

"I only been here two days," the man whined.

"That's long enough for you to learn something. Talk, fella, *talk!* Unless you want things to happen!"

Morton stood on one side, shaking his gray head. Morton, more than twice his partner's age, didn't believe in rough stuff—usually. He had no *moral* objection to it. He simply thought that, as a rule, it didn't get you anywhere. And he warned McGarvey that this prisoner was notoriously tough. He could take anything. But McGarvey wouldn't believe that.

And the funny part of it was, McGarvey was proving to be correct! After nothing worse than slaps and bluster, the man was babbling!

Morton thought: Has this guy lost his nerve since I questioned him two years ago? There's something funny about this.

McGarvey, flushed and triumphant, cried, "You told us everything, huh? Well, maybe this will remind you of something more!"

His fist swung back. It was to have been a punch to the chest. Not a hard punch—McGarvey could have splintered the man's ribs—but a stiff, thudding "reminder," that was all.

Its effect was extraordinary. The cracksman's eyes flew wide open and sheer panic blazed in them. His jaw fell. Every speck of color went out of his thick, sweating face.

His lips moved, but there was only a thin, whistling, throaty sound.

Morton sprang forward, grabbed his partner's wrist, lifted the blow so that it passed over the prisoner's shoulder.

"What the—" McGarvey began.

"You knocked him out."

"Knocked him *out!* Why, I didn't even touch him!"

"No, but you were going to. And he's fainted."

"Say, I thought you told me this guy was tough?"

Morton said, "Maybe we didn't frisk him right. That poke would have landed right here—" His fingers went underneath the prisoner's coat on the right side, then under the shirt. "You would have hit this—"

Out of a concealed pocket he took a stoppered test-tube filled with some grayish, opaque liquid.

"Maybe that rough stuff is good sometimes after all," he mused. "He didn't want us to find this, and we wouldn't have found it if you hadn't swung your fist that way. That was why he talked so much. He was afraid you'd hit his chest. And when you started one there, he fainted."

"What— Well, what the hell *is* that stuff anyway?"

"Only nitroglycerin," said Morton.

NOBODY AROUND HEADQUARTERS at the time was quite certain whether the fluid constituted a "burglar's tool" in the eyes of the law, or whether it would be necessary to bring a charge of transporting explosives without a license. Possibly, somebody suggested, both raps might be made to stick. Meanwhile the pickup was officially and conveniently classed as a "vagrant," and locked up; and Morton and McGarvey, washing their hands of him, went forth into the chilly, rainy afternoon to check the tips he had blurted.

They went to a certain room in a certain hotel. They knocked; and when somebody called to ask who was there, young McGarvey replied in a fairly boyish soprano, "Telegram for you, sir." The door was opened, and a man said, "Oh," looking sore.

"Hello, Daly. The mustache is an improvement. Keeping busy?"

"I just got here this morning."

"We know that," said Morton.

"You got nothing on me! I'm not wanted anywhere!"

"You're certainly not wanted here," Morton agreed. He handed the man a time-table. "There's three trains between now and midnight, Daly. We don't care which one you take."

"Say, you can't pull that stuff—"

"I've told the house dick, and he's agreed to go with you to the station in case you need anybody to carry your bag. Or even if you don't."

They went out, McGarvey, swaggering a little. They went to a small house in South Miami Avenue, where they interrupted five men who were shooting craps. Just a friendly game, the men said. Morton said he was sure it was, and here were five time-tables.

While he was handing these out, grave as ever, quiet-voiced, he saw a sixth man reflected in the glass over a picture. He wheeled, putting his right hand to the butt of his gun.

"Don't do that!" he said.

The sixth man, who had crept in from the kitchen, held

a footstool which he had raised above the unsuspecting McGarvey's head. Now he froze in that position. He was no fool, and he'd heard how Wentworth L. Morton could shoot.

McGarvey turned, bellowing.

"Interfering with an officer in pursuit of his duty!" he howled.

McGarvey hit the man on the chin, and the man went over backward, footstool and all, over a rocking chair. It made a lot of noise, and smashed the rocking chair.

McGarvey, his back up, would have gone around slugging all the others; but Morton called him off.

"Save your knuckles. And if we did pinch that guy, all five of his pals here would swear that you started it. Not worth the trouble." He said to the five crap shooters, "There's three trains before midnight. And there's two men in a car at the end of this block who'll count you out and trail you to the station and see that you get your tickets and tuck you into your Pullman seats. Come on, Garv."

They went to a cheap furnished apartment house in Northeast Fourth Street not far from the Boulevard.

"Who is this guy Stanley?" McGarvey asked.

"George Stanley. He's a Greek. Right name is Stanipopulous or something. Specializes in gypping his fellow countrymen who don't know the language. Collects moneys for funds that never existed, and sells phony seats on the Stock Exchange, and issues fake naturalization papers. He's a born louse. No guts, and he'd do anything in the world for money. Especially if he can get it from some poor Dago who spent all his life working for it."

"I'd like to take a poke at a guy like that."

"You take too many pokes," Morton grumbled. "Besides, this baby's soft. He'll run out of town when we say 'boo' to him."

HE RANG THE bell marked "Allen," this being another item of information disgorged by the safe-cracker. There was no answer. But somebody was just quitting the house, and McGarvey caught the door while it was open; and they went in anyway. They went up to Apartment 22. They knocked, and got no answer. The door was ajar. They went in.

It was a small and shabbily furnished apartment. A shredded straw rug had been kicked into a corner. A chair was overturned. An ashtray had been knocked off the table.

"Two different kinds of cigarettes," Morton remarked.

"He must have had a friend here."

"More likely a victim. Stanley isn't the kind of a guy who would have any friends."

Morton started out. But he paused in the doorway, frowning.

McGarvey asked, "What's the matter?"

"I don't know... Something funny about this place."

They searched the apartment thoroughly. There was no evidence that any more than one man was occupying it. There was one razor in the bathroom, and one toothbrush.

"He certainly wouldn't have left them," said Morton, "if he'd been tipped off that we were coming. No matter how fast a man scrams he's going to at least take his toothbrush."

Dust was thick on the floor, except in one corner where there was a clear space about twenty inches square.

*"Interfering with an officer
in pursuit of his duty!"*

"Somebody's picked up a box or something from here...."

McGarvey complained, "I don't see how that gets us anywhere."

"Neither do I."

"What are you looking for then?"

"I don't know. It's just that there's something funny about this place. I can just sort of *smell* something wrong."

"Well, take your time. Don't mind me! It's raining now anyway."

Morton went over the whole apartment again. He was as serious as a priest, as thorough as a scientist. But at last he shook his head. He said "All right," and they started out.

Yet even in the hallway Morton was troubled. He couldn't seem to leave that hallway.

"Let's give a knock next door here and see if they heard anything funny," he suggested.

He knocked on the door of Apartment 23. There was no answer. He tried the knob. The door was locked.

"I don't know what I'm doing this for," Morton admitted, and his tone was querulous, as though he were impatient with himself for indulging in such foolishness, "but I'm going to have a look in this apartment, too."

He had a large bunch of skeleton keys, and it was a simple, old-fashioned lock and not strong. Soon he opened the door.

A couple of less case-hardened men might have turned and run. Even young McGarvey, who had a strong stomach, leaned against the door and swallowed hard several times, and his face went white.

The man had been at least seventy years old, short, but of distinguished appearance. His clothes were expensive. His white buckskin sport shoes alone must have cost twenty-five dollars. They hung about ten inches from the floor.

He had a small, round, cherubic face. Normally, you suspected, it would have been pink. Just now it was blue, a very dark blue which looked even darker in contrast with the handsome white beard. The lips, too, were blue, though they were flecked by white foam. Between them a bluish tongue protruded.

All windows were closed in this apartment, but the body swayed the least bit in the stir of air created when Morton opened the door.

YOUNG McGARVEY RECOVERED himself, squeezed past his partner, went toward the corpse. He was muttering something, and pulling a penknife from his pocket.

Morton called sharply, "Don't cut him down!"

"But the guy's—"

"He's as dead now as he's ever going to be. And I don't want him touched until the photographers get here."

The body had stopped swaying. Morton went to it, tapped the face with one finger, remarked that it was still warm. He encircled it, looking at everything but touching nothing. He even got flat on his back on the floor, and worked his head underneath the feet. He was as deliberate as an anthropologist who examines a strange skeleton.

When Morton got up, McGarvey stammered:

"You know—you know who I think this is, Mort?"

Morton nodded. "Yes, I think so."

With two fingers he went into the man's inner coat pocket. He drew out a few letters, glanced at the addresses, nodded, and with two fingers put them back where he'd found them.

"Yes," he said. "It's old Sam T. Packhard himself. I read in the *Herald* today where he'd come to town."

"Cripes," muttered young McGarvey.

For there were few greater names than that of Samuel Tertius Packhard. He was more than a multi-millionaire; he was a myth. One of the most sensational and most successful of the rugged individualists, he had piled up an immense fortune; and then he had retired. He was a reminder of a past Wall Street generation. He had been rich at twenty-eight. At fifty he was being investigated by the United States Senate, and I.W.W. fanatics were trying to toss bombs at him. At seventy-two he was a dim, benevolent figure, living in remote splendor, endowing hospitals and universities and libraries. He seldom appeared in the newspapers any longer, and most persons found it difficult to believe he was still alive. He had not even issued a statement about the depression.

McGarvey pointed to an overturned chair.

"See, there's the scuffs the bottom of his shoes made when he kicked it out from under him."

"Those are sport shoes," Morton said tonelessly, "and they have rubber soles and heels."

"Huh?"

"Get down there and look, if you don't believe me. And another thing—come here."

The rope was slim, new, hempen, yellow. One end of it had been fastened in a noose around Packhard's neck. It went up over an ornamental wooden crosspiece between the living room and the kitchen, and then down into the kitchen, the other end being tied firmly to a hook in the wall.

Morton said, "Look at it here in the kitchen. You figure he fastened that end here, and then threw the other end over that beam, and then got up on a chair and made a noose and hanged himself, eh? All right. Then how does it happen that the fibres of loose hemp on the under side in here all point *up?*"

There was a scowl of perplexity on McGarvey's face.

"I don't get it."

"That rope's been pulled over something. Pulled hard. Which is why the fibers are all stroked that way—*up.*"

"Meaning?"

"Meaning that this man didn't hang himself. The noose was put around his neck and he was *pulled* up to that position."

2

"IT'S MURDER!"

SAMUEL TERTIUS PACKHARD had been a widower, and childless. His principal heir, the man who for some years had run his entire estate, was his nephew, Vaughan Packhard. Vaughan Packhard was in Miami. But Morton and McGarvey didn't go directly to the home he had shared with his uncle. They started for it; but near Flagler Street the older detective said suddenly:

"Pull up in front of the Ponce de Leon Trust here a minute."

"What's this?"

"Hunch," said Morton. "Nothing but a hunch."

They cornered a vice-president, an acquaintance of Morton, who tried to be friendly, though he was awed by Morton's solemn manner. Yes, the vice-president said, Mr. Packhard had an account at this bank.

Morton asked, "Was he here today?"

The vice-president looked at McGarvey.

Morton asked again, "Was he here today? Did he draw anything?"

The vice-president, still looking at McGarvey, said, "Sergeant, I'm not sure that it would be proper for me to answer that question."

Morton said, "Mr. Welsh, I think you better answer it. If you're worried about Garv, all right. I can send him out on something else. For instance, did Sam T. Packhard leave in one of his own cars?"

"No, it was a taxi."

"Then he *was* here!" Morton turned to his partner. "Get that cab driver, kid." And when McGarvey had gone, Morton said again, "I think you better answer that question, Mr. Welsh."

Morton knew very little. He was guessing. But he *seemed* to know a lot. He had a wonderful way of getting facts out of people.

Ten minutes later, on the sidewalk, he was getting a few additional facts out of a taxi driver. Then he climbed back into the department car.

McGarvey asked, "You find out anything inside there?"

"Plenty." Morton was thoughtful. "Now we go to the Packhard mansion. You know where it is?"

"Who doesn't?"

When they turned into an imposing driveway, Morton said, "I understand this Vaughan Packhard is a disagreeable guy. And this time I think I'll leave you outside."

McGarvey blustered, "What's the big idea?"

"Well, if you must know, I'm afraid you'll start yelling and make him freeze up. There's something I want to get out of Vaughan Packhard, and if I don't get it now I never will. Pretty soon this house we're coming to is going to be practically in a state of siege. Reporters and picture men will be here from all over the country, and then Vaughan Packhard's going to be harder to get at than the Pope. We're first on the scene, and I want to take advantage of it."

"Now listen, Mort! If you can't trust me with anything—"

"I'll trust you with lots, kid, but not with this."

A disapproving butler said, "Please wait here for a moment." And presently a tall, brittle man with a lean blue chin hurried into the reception room.

"What is this, Sergeant? Has anything happened to old Mr. Packhard? I'm his secretary, Mr. Charlot."

"You're no secretary," Morton said. "You're a cop."

The tall man flushed.

"Well, it's true I was a policeman at one time, but—now see here, I'll admit I've lost track of old Mr. Packhard, and if you gentlemen know anything—"

"So you're a bodyguard?" Morton never had liked private detectives, and he wouldn't have liked this one under any circumstances. "Well, you must be a lousy one then."

"Now damn it, Sergeant! I'm not going to stand here and—" He pulled himself together. He was frightened. "Has anything happened?"

"Nothing much. Except that your boss just got murdered."

"Murdered! Good God! Mur—"

The butler had reappeared. Morton stepped past Charlot. But the bodyguard turned, grabbed Morton's left sleeve.

"Now wait a minute, Sergeant! Before you see Mr. Vaughan Packhard I'd like to speak to you for a minute."

Morton walked toward the butler. Charlot cried:

"Well then, suppose I go in with you?"

"Suppose you stay out here." Morton's gray eyes, ordinarily thoughtful and benign, shrieked slaughter now. "You mussed your job, so now don't come whimpering to me about it! I'll see Mr. Vaughan Packhard by himself, and you'll stay out here."

"Yes," said McGarvey, "you'll stay out here."

"Say, do you realize you're in a private residence?" the secretary blustered.

"I can hit just as hard in a private residence as I can outside," said young McGarvey. "Want me to prove it?"

VAUGHAN PACKHARD WAS a tense, chill man in his lower fifties. He thought in terms of money. He moved money, controlled money, watched money, and cared for nothing else. He did not make any pretense of having an interest in art or science or charity. He was not unique. He was simply a hard, an extraordinarily hard business man. His uncle, for years hailed as one of the most brilliant minds in American finance, had amassed a monstrous fortune; and while Vaughan Packhard administered this he never had tried to make any notable increases in it—that would have been beyond his power—but he kept it intact.

He sat now at a Renaissance desk. You knew it was a desk because there was an inkstand on it, and a wine-colored blotter.

Wentworth L. Morton told the story in a simple, undramatic fashion. Packhard, a pale man anyway, grew paler, almost white. But he didn't tremble. The story finished, he rose and went to a window. He stood there a moment; and when he turned there was fine perspiration on his forehead and on his upper lip, and the veins in his temples were pounding, yet his face remained expressionless.

"Are you absolutely certain it was not suicide?"

"Absolutely. The fibers on the under side of the rope show that the body was pulled up to that position. And besides, there was no key in the apartment, or in any of Mr. Packhard's pockets, and yet the door was locked. He couldn't have locked himself in and then thrown the key out of a window, because the windows haven't been touched in months."

"But you can't hang a man alive!"

"You can if he's been knocked out. He might have been smacked on the chin, and it wouldn't show bruises because of the whiskers. Or he might have been choked first, or strangled. The appearance of the body would be exactly the same."

Vaughan Packhard exhaled a little.

"Thank God for that," he muttered.

"If that sounds callous, officer," he added earnestly, "you must realize that I'm obliged to think of the effect the suicide of a man like Samuel T. Packhard would have upon the money market. Some of our biggest holdings are in none too good condition as it is, and my uncle, though he was supposed to have retired, still held control of those securities in his own name." He stopped, rubbing his hands together.

Morton said, "He went to the Ponce de Leon Trust and cashed his personal check for fifty thousand less than an hour before we found him. They gave him the money wrapped up in brown paper. We've talked to the cab driver who drove him out to this apartment house. Your uncle had been there before, evidently. He rang a bell without stopping to read names. And the catch clicked right away, and he went in."

"Did you find the money?"

"No. Nor the wrapper. But it was in fifties and one

hundreds the bank had just received, and we got the numbers. When that money begins to show up, we'll learn something. Meanwhile," said Morton, "it would help if you'd explain why your uncle had a bodyguard."

"Oh, you met Charlot? Why, we've had him four years now. Thought it safest. All this kidnaping going on and everything."

"Had your uncle ever received a kidnap threat?"

"Well, no. But we thought it best not to take any chances."

"Had he ever been threatened with blackmail?"

"Of course not! His life is certainly well enough known to make such an idea preposterous! He was a highly moral man. He was one of the biggest contributors to the Anti-Saloon League and the Anti-Tobacco League and the—"

"I know all that." Morton rose, leaned over the desk. "But just the same he had a bodyguard. Or was that guy a nurse maybe?"

"See here, what are you—"

"Listen, your uncle's mind had failed some time ago, hadn't it? Only you didn't get him declared legally insane because you were afraid you couldn't keep it out of the papers, which might have a bad effect on your holdings."

"That's an absolute lie!"

"Would you swear to that before a grand jury?"

"I'll swear I threw you out of this house because you had the—"

There was a terrific thud in the reception room. The windows rattled. Morton cried, "Damnation!" and ran to the door and threw it open. Young McGarvey, his face brick-red, his fists clenched, stood over an emphatically horizontal Charlot.

"You ape! I'm just beginning to get somewhere when you got to start slugging people!" Morton said.

"This rat had the nerve to try to get me to swear that the taxi driver was lying when he said that—" McGarvey began.

"Never mind! Never mind! It's too late now!"

Servants were appearing in doorways. Vaughan Pack-hard, who'd taken one look at his late uncle's bodyguard, was shouting into a telephone, "Operator, I want a police station!" Morton, sighing, crossed the reception room, took his partner's arm.

"He wanted to bribe me, the dirty lousy—"

"Shut up! You've made enough noise already. Come on."

3

McGARVEY ON HIS OWN

ON THE WAY back to headquarters young McGarvey, driving savagely, was silent. He worshiped Morton, always had worshiped him; Morton had been his boyhood hero. But right now, because he was excited, he was furious. He hated to be treated like a child.

And Morton too—Morton was sore. He liked this kid, liked him a lot, and had high hopes for him. He's been in tight places with young McGarvey, and he knew how the boy could fight. But sometimes he despaired of ever jamming any sense into that big bull-like head.

This had been a long time coming, this difference. It had been in the cards. Morton had been growing more and more crabby, young McGarvey more impatient and more cocky, as success followed success.

McGarvey parked the car very carefully; and instead of leaping out, as he usually did, he turned to his partner.

"Listen, Mort. I hate like hell to say this."

"Go ahead, say it! Don't mind me!"

"Well then, if you think I'm going to stand around saying 'yes' to you all my life, and having you treat me like a—"

A patrolman interrupted them. He must have heard them quarreling, and certainly he wouldn't have dared to break in on Morton and McGarvey that way—unless it was important.

Morton snarled, "What the hell do you want?"

"Sorry, Sergeant, but it's—it's—"

"Well, what *is* it?"

"It's a murder! Upper end of Bayfront Park! Captain Montgomery just called and said to tell you the victim is George Stanley!"

The little skin game artist from Greece was sprawled on his face behind a hibiscus hedge, and his hands, stretched above his head, seemed to be trying to grip the wet grass. His head was mostly blood mixed with rainwater.

There were many cops there, and they were holding the crowd back. The park, understandably, was not popular on a rainy evening. The danger was rather that the cops themselves would trample upon evidence. Captain Montgomery, who was keeping a watchful eye on them, nodded with relief when Morton appeared.

"Doc hasn't arrived yet. It *is* Stanley, isn't it?"

Morton said, "Yes. They been marching back and forth?"

"Some. But I stopped them as soon as I got here."

The ground around the body, being soft from rain, was covered with footprints, but most of these were irregular, slurred.

Morton turned to his partner, "We've got to see if any of these match up with the ones in that apartment. Run back to headquarters and get me that spray gun in the bottom of the closet and all the blotters you can corral. Also I want a can of shellac and a big can of talcum powder and the plaster of Paris that's in my locker. And make it fast."

McGarvey swallowed, inhaled tremblingly, and his eyes got very small. But he went away without a word.

Morton stood there staring at the corpse.

"Search him?" he said to the policeman.

"Yes. No money. No watch. No nothing, in fact."

Morton's gaze moved here and there.

"You don't seem surprised," Montgomery offered.

"I'd only be surprised," said Morton, "if we'd found this guy alive."

When his partner returned, and handed over the material, Morton went to work on the footprints. First he blotted out as much of the water as he could. Then he sprinkled talcum powder very lightly into the prints, and over this, using the spray gun, he sprayed a fine film of shellac. Another layer of powder. Another film of shellac. He fitted each print with at least three coatings of each material before he ventured to fill it with plaster of Paris.

It was a long job and a hard one, but Morton did it without a word, without even looking up. He had a large audience, but he paid it no attention. He worked, scarcely pausing even to kick the kinks out of his legs, until well after midnight; and when finally he straightened he had, in addition to five failures which he broke, nine perfect casts, each one showing every mark of sole and heel, every scuffed spot, every nail and thread.

"Well, now if we catch 'em we can convict 'em," he muttered. "But of course the thing is to catch 'em first. Take good care of these things, will you, Monty? I'm going to bed."

He left without a word to his partner; and young McGarvey, glowering, didn't say a word to him.

THEY HAD IT out next morning before Captain Montgomery, who, listening to both of them, puffed a cigar methodically, gingerly, as though he didn't enjoy it, but thought smoking was expected of him.

"Well, that's the way it is," McGarvey finished. "Mort says I'm a nuisance and I always spoil things, and if he feels that way about it, all right! If he'd only open up sometimes, and tell me what he's doing, maybe I could be some help."

"Yes," said Montgomery, nodding sympathetically. "Yes, I know how he is. He never tells me anything either, and I'm his boss."

"I was on the edge of getting somewhere with that guy Packhard," Morton said bitterly. "Well, you saw how it was when we were able to question him again, Monty? Lawyers and secretaries and private dicks all over the place!"

"Yes," said Montgomery, "we didn't learn much, that's a fact."

McGarvey blurted, "Maybe I'm not such a lousy detective after all!"

"Nobody said you were lousy, Garv," the Captain purred.

"Maybe if I had my own way about a few things I could find this guy we're looking for myself!"

"What guy is that?"

"Why, this guy that must have been in the apartment with Stanley. There were two different kinds of butts there, and certainly Sam T. Packhard never smoked in his life. So there must have been another guy. Him and Stanley hung Packhard, in the next apartment, and then the other guy got Stanley outside and slapped his skull in. He'd be another confidence man probably. A slick guy, and a flashy dresser."

The captain asked Morton, who was looking out a window, "That who you're looking for, Mort?"

Without moving, Morton said, "No."

"Who is it you're looking for, Mort?"

"Thank goodness we've got a clear day today anyway," Morton said, "after all that rain."

"You *see?* That's the way he always is!" McGarvey said.

"And that's the way he always has been," Montgomery said sadly, "as long as I've known him, which is a long, long while."

Morton said, "Of course this flashy dresser's going to go right out and start spending that fifty grand, now that somebody's told reporters about it and the papers are carrying the numbers of the bills. Sure."

McGarvey flushed. "All right, maybe that was dumb," he admitted.

"Maybe?"

McGarvey trembled, and his face gleamed with sweat. Nobody else would have dared to talk to him that way. But after a moment, during which nobody stirred, he turned again to the captain.

"Well," he said, "what are you going to do about it?"

Montgomery was a Solomon, smooth and fat, sage, diplomatic, amiable. He placed the cigar in an ashtray.

"Well, here's what I think. Suppose Mort goes on looking for whoever it is he's looking for, and you go on looking for whoever it is *you're* looking for. We'll make a little race of it, maybe, and see who wins. The reporters will just figure that the two of you are checking each other's stuff. Okay?"

McGarvey cried, "Suits me! That's all I ever asked was a chance to go out and investigate a thing the way I want."

He fairly ran for the door. "I'm starting right now!" He slammed the door after him.

4

MORTON FINDS A BOX

MONTGOMERY SAT LOOKING glumly at the remains of the cigar, then at the row of plaster of Paris footprint moulds on his desk.

"He's a good kid at that," he said finally. "Shame he thinks he's so hot. He isn't right about that pal of Stanley's, is he?"

Morton moved to a chair, lighted a cigar of his own.

"No. It would have taken two men to haul Sam Packhard up off the floor, and Stanley wouldn't have been one because he wouldn't have had the nerve. Those butts in the ashtray were Camels and Luckies, and the analysis of the tobacco crumbs in Stanley's pocket shows he smoked Chesterfields. He wouldn't be smoking anyway when he had a date with Sam Packhard. He'd know how the old man detested cigarettes.

"Also," Morton went on, "there's the footprints. And the marks on his skull show that Stanley was smacked on both sides of the head at practically the same instant. Otherwise he wouldn't have bled so much. He was hit by something smallish on the left side and something pretty heavy on the right. Might have been the barrel of a big gun and the barrel of a little gun, or it might have been a gun on one side and a blackjack on the other, or a piece of pipe and a blackjack—that part doesn't matter. The point is that he was killed by at least two men. And I think a third one was there carrying a big square box. There wasn't any mark of such a box being put down there anywhere."

Montgomery glanced at the door.

"If that kid ever does happen to stumble into something—"he began slowly.

"You know," Morton said, "he's got just enough dumb Irish luck to maybe do a thing like that. It would be a shame. The newspapers would make a hero out of him all over again, and he'd get such a swelled head he never would be much good any more."

"Maybe you better go out and clean it up yourself, Mort."

Morton sighed, and rose.

"Maybe I'd better, at that," he said.

Wentworth L. Morton worked on the case five days. There isn't much use telling in detail what he did, for it was all straight detective work, which is the dullest work in the world.

He had almost nothing to go on. Hundreds of persons, possibly thousands, were pouring into Miami every day, and Morton could not even be sure that the two or three men he sought were still in Florida. He didn't know their names. He had no personal descriptions. Because they had known George Stanley, he assumed that at least one of them, and probably both or all, were Greeks. There were no foreign language newspapers published in or near Miami, yet none of the missing money had showed up anywhere, so it was reasonable to suppose that at least one of the men was able to read English. If they remained in the city, they were certainly broke and friendless. From the nature of the murders Morton felt sure that the men were stupid, headstrong, and very tough indeed.

The section of Bayfront Park in which Stanley's body was found was near the end of Fourth Street, not far from the apartment house in which Sam T. Packhard was hanged. So presumably the men did not have a car. If they'd had a car they would have selected a more remote spot. Just this fact, then, was a help. Morton did not go to any garage, parking lot or service station.

But he went almost everywhere else. He started at the park, and walked this way and that, asking questions. He knew scores of people, hundreds of people, for he'd lived in Miami all his life, and knowing people who might notice things was part of his business. So he went around asking questions. Two men or three, dark-haired, tough and dumb and not well-dressed, and one of them carrying a large square box.

He would work back to the park, then start all over again. He never hurried, never got excited. When reporters found him, as they did from time to time, he stalled them, slipped away from them; he wouldn't tell anything.

Young McGarvey, he saw by the papers, was doing plenty of talking, running down plenty of clues. Young McGarvey still was seeking that flashily dressed Greek. He was making arrests by the dozen—and turning all the prisoners loose again after a few hours of questioning. Oh, he was busy! He had even raided a poolroom and two petty gambling games; they were one-man raids, very rough; and as a result of them—the only result—he had locked up seven no-account tin-horns on charges of interfering with an officer in the performance of his duty.

MORTON, STAID AND stolid, mooched around asking questions. And on the fifth day, early in the evening, he found the murderers' hide-out.

He didn't know it was the place he sought. It was only another bungalow which according to his informant housed three dark-haired strangers; and Miami was filled with strangers. Morton had tried scores of other places just like this one.

But he was in the Southwest Twenties, near the Tami-ami Trail. Somewhere in this neighborhood three men with a large square box had been seen. He was getting close to them—if they were the right men.

He plodded up a path to the tiny house. He was tired, sweaty, rather shabby. Seeing him, you would have supposed him too weary to be interested in anything at all. But in fact he was alert. The men he was after were fools, yes; but fools can be dangerous. You never know what a fool is going to do. And if even a half-wit points a gun at you and pulls the trigger, that little chunk of lead performs exactly the same function as though an intellectual wizard had sent it on its way.

He rang the bell. He heard somebody move around inside, but there was no answer. He rang again. Somebody called: "Who is it?"

"Florida Power and Light Company," Morton answered.

It got dark abruptly, as it does in tropical and semi-tropical countries, where there never is much twilight. Insects were droning among the weeds of the little lawn.

"What d'yuh want?"

"Look at your meter."

"Our lights are all right here."

"They won't be, if you don't let me read that meter! They'll be shut off on you!"

He could hear whispering. He yawned, looked out over the quiet street. The door opened an inch or two.

"How do we know you're really from the light people?"

Dumb, Morton thought. He produced a card.

"This satisfy you?"

A hand came out, disappeared with the card. The door was closed and locked. Morton waited patiently. He knew the credentials were good. He'd used them before.

The door was opened again.

"All right. Come on in. It's in the kitchen."

He was familiar with this type of house. A front door opening directly into a medium-sized living room. Beyond that a small bedroom. Beyond the bedroom a kitchen, and on the left a bath. That was all there was to the place.

All shades were drawn, but in the dim living room, as he heard the door closed behind him, he could distinguish two pairs of eyes, one near the front window, one back by the bedroom. He had to pass within a few inches of the man near the bedroom.

He kicked the end of the bed as he passed it. It was low—too low, he estimated, to hide a box under.

"Don't you believe in light in this place?" he grumbled. **HE PRODUCED A** flashlight. Every meter inspector should carry a flashlight; but the one Morton had was far bigger and stronger than the usual kind.

Somebody behind him was breathing heavily.

Morton put the flashlight under his left arm, read the

meter, and jotted down some figures in a notebook. He neither hurried nor did he stall.

"Okay," he said, and put the notebook and pencil away.

Then he turned in such a way that the flash swept the whole of the kitchen. No square box there. No place for one.

The man who had been behind him stepped back into the bedroom.

"This practically finishes me for the day," Morton told nobody in particular. "Only got a couple of more houses."

The flashlight was in his left hand now. He went through the bedroom, getting a fair glimpse of it and of the man in it. The man was dark and small, and looked like a Greek.

In the living room he stumbled. He seemed to have some difficulty catching his balance, and for a moment the flashlight beam swung wildly back and forth.

"It's none of my business, of course, but you aren't saving much on your bills by keeping the place as dark as this."

He had not obtained a good look at either of the two men in the living room, but he had seen the box. It was in a corner—a box about twenty-six inches square, about eighteen inches high, with shiny gadgets on the top and in one side a small rectangle of glass.

It was enough. Until this time it would have been risky to bring a squad to this house. He might get into a lot of trouble doing that, or at the very least make a damned fool of himself. But now he knew where he stood. He had no intention of tackling these three men himself! He was too old to care for physical danger; he was too sensible. He'd get plenty of help, and get it right away.

Somebody said, "Wait a minute. Let's see that paper again."

Morton grunted. "What do you think I am, anyway? I haven't got all night!"

Somebody bumped against him from behind. A pair of hands brushed his right hip.

Somebody else bumped him from the left. He carried his pistol on his left, at the waist, ready for a cross-belly draw.

A voice said, "Is that a gun you got there, fella?"

"Sure it's a gun! We always carry a gun, all meter inspectors."

He was within a few inches of the front door, and reaching for the knob, when something hit him just above the kidneys.

"This is a gun too. Better stick your hands up."

After that his act was spoiled. Not caring for suicide, he raised his hands. Men he couldn't see patted him, felt his pockets, found the badge pinned inside his coat. A match flared. The pressure on Morton's back remained the same. The match went out.

"Yeah, that's what he is. He's a cop."

5

MORTON TAKES IT ALONE

HE EXPECTED A beating, at first, and stolidly he waited for it. Despite his appearance—put a turned-around collar on him and he could have passed for a clergyman—Morton had taken more than one beating in his time. And given more than one, too.

But the men were cool. They took his gun, they snapped on the lights, and they stood in front of him looking at him. Two of them had guns. These two were short swarthy men with great shoulders and thick heads and very narrow eyes. They looked curiously alike. Twins maybe; certainly brothers anyway. The third was tall, husky, with long arms, shaggy black eyebrows which met in the middle, and the complexion of an olive seen through a bad Martini. They were not the current gangster type, not silk-shirted kids with highly manicured nails; they were men in their upper thirties—laboring men, maybe dishwashers or bartenders or truck drivers.

"What are you doing here, copper?"

"What do you think I'm doing?" Morton's voice was calm.

"Reading the meter; I suppose?"

"Well, I did read it, didn't I?"

The tall man with one backward swipe of his hand knocked the Panama off Morton's head. Morton didn't stir.

"I know who he is now! He's that Sergeant Morton that's supposed to be so smart."

"He *must* be smart to walk in here alone like this."

There was no expression on Morton's face, but he was cursing himself for being so damned secretive. Any other cop would have arranged to have somebody with him, or at least behind him, checking his movements. But Morton always had preferred to do things alone, trusting nobody and confiding in nobody, until he had his case completed. Sometimes that was a good idea, and sometimes it wasn't. He had his case completed now—but was it too late? Probably.

This was the close-mouthness of which McGarvey had complained. And Morton was wondering now, facing the Greeks, whether young McGarvey wasn't right. He certainly wished he had Garv with him. For McGarvey didn't know the meaning of fear, or even, despite Morton's teachings, of ordinary caution; McGarvey, in a fight, seemed like a herd of enraged Texas longhorns.

But McGarvey wasn't here.

The three men were talking among themselves in Greek now, but their gestures were easily understood. They were trying to decide what to do with Morton. They didn't wish to shoot him because a shot would be heard. If they cracked his skull with gun butts, they'd still have a body on their hands. And no car. They couldn't run away from Miami— at least, not far away—because they didn't have enough money.

To be sure, they had fifty thousand in good hard cash.

But it was in fifty and one-hundred dollar bills, and all the numbers had been published. They didn't dare pass one of those bills. The money they had taken from Morton's pockets didn't help much. It was only $2.37. Probably they had planned to wait in this house, keeping utterly quiet, as long as their funds lasted. Probably they had hoped that by that time the search for the stolen bills would have cooled. It wasn't like being in New York and taking a tube to Jersey City, or being in Washington and hopping a bus for Baltimore. Miami is a long distance from any other large center of population, and these men would be conspicuous in any place which was not a large center of population.

Even Morton had never before realized how a modern gunman is lost without an automobile.

One of the short fellows indicated the bedroom. "Back there, copper," he said.

As he obeyed, Morton saw the big fellow go to a front window, while the other man slipped outside.

His captor switched on the light and made Morton lie on his back on the bed. He himself stood at the foot of the bed.

Morton asked indifferently, "What did you have against George Stanley? Or was it an ordinary muscle-in job?"

"That rat! He gypped us in Philadelphia! Every dollar we have! We work for years, save up money to go back to the old country—and he comes along and steals it all!"

AFTER A TIME the other short man returned by the back door. He seemed satisfied that there were no policemen outside. He and his brother stood close together, glaring at the recumbent detective, and talking in low rapid voices, in Greek.

Then the first man moved to the right of Morton, the second moved to the left. His eyes followed them. The first man, the man who had conducted Morton into the bedroom, kept his pistol pointed at Morton's chest. It was a Savage .32 pocket automatic, a ten-shooter they don't make any more. The man thumbed off the safety. His eyes were black, snake-like, and seemed never to blink.

The other man was drawing a monstrous army automatic, a .45 Colt. They make wonderful clubs, those government guns.

The man with the Savage shifted that weapon to his left hand and put his right hand into a coat pocket. A blackjack?

"Sit up," this man commanded. "We want to take you out."

Morton knew what was going to happen. The instant he sat up he'd get it from one side or the other, depending upon which way he turned. Perhaps he'd get it from both sides at once.

"Sit up. We ain't going to hurt you."

Morton managed a smile. "Oh, I'm sure you're not," he murmured.

He was tense, with no plan of action. He was simply going to try to grab the wrist of the first man who swung on him and then try to roll out of the way of the blow from the other side. But it wouldn't last long, he knew, no matter how he fought.

"All right then. If you want to be that way about it, *take it lying down!*"

Morton jerked his head away from the sound of that voice—and something heavy thumped the pillow at his right ear. He jerked his head back, rolled, raised his arms. The blows were coming from both sides now. One of them paralyzed his right arm for an instant, and a gun butt swished past his right forehead as he rolled again.

One of the men was cursing slowly, feelingly, in a low monotone. The other said nothing at all. They were both breathing hard.

Morton's arms were jerked down by the man on the right. He ducked. What seemed like a sledge hammer struck the back of his neck; an inch higher and it would have cracked his skull.

Now he was stunned, but he fought on. He slipped the grip of the man who held his arms, launched a kick at that man's chest, wriggled sideways.... But from the other side the butt of the big Colt found his skull.

Long red and yellow streamers swirled through a roaring sky of black. Swirled, collected, exploded like rockets. The blackness faded, the red too, and through a gauzy haze of yellow Morton saw the two men closing in on him again, their weapons raised. He was, in that instant, helpless. Literally he couldn't have moved to save his life.

From the living room came a frightened, urgent whisper: "Hey, there's somebody coming up to the house!"

The yellowish haze thinned. Morton saw the two brothers look at one another. They were panting, sweating.

From the living room, "He's a great big guy. Must be six feet four. All by himself."

Morton's heart sang, and his blood ran fast. Was it possible that that brass-headed, steel-fisted, stubborn son of an Irishman had by some streak of the mad luck for which he was famous, stumbled upon this place? It would be like young McGarvey to come striding in alone, utterly confident that he could round up a whole mob single-handed. Or did he think he was about to arrest a mere confidence man?

Or maybe it was somebody else, and not McGarvey at all?

The man with the Savage jerked his head toward the living room, and said to his brother, "Go stand behind the door. If it's a cop, and he tries to get in, let it fly! We'll polish off this baby afterward."

6

SECRET CARGO

FROM THE BEDROOM they could hear the knocking.

"Who is it?"

"Open up. I want to ask you something."

Morton knew that voice. McGarvey!

There was some silence; then the door was opened.

"What d'yuh want?"

Morton heard his partner say, "Sorry to bother you, buddy, but I'm looking for a guy that's around reading electric meters. He been here? A guy in his fifties, with gray hair. Moves slow and don't talk much."

The man with Morton had raised his head, listening, and instinctively his eyes rolled in the direction of the living room. The barrel of the Savage—the muzzle was about four feet from Morton's chest—moved so that it was pointed a little to the right. A shot now would still catch Morton in the right lung, probably, but it was worth a chance. And Morton would have taken that chance, except that there was young McGarvey to think of.

"Him? Yeah, he was here about half an hour ago."

"Which way did he go?"

"I didn't notice, buddy."

"Oh. Well, much obliged," McGarvey's voice sounded disappointed.

"Don't mention it, buddy."

The door was closed. And Morton sprang.

He came off the bed in one bound, twisting to the left and bringing his left hand down on the barrel of the Savage. His right hand he slapped underneath the butt. He pushed away from the bed, throwing the gun up. It exploded twice, and the third time the hammer caught the loose skin between the thumb and forefinger of his left hand. It gave him such a shock of pain that his grip slipped. His hands were wet with sweat anyway.

He had been trying to get his left leg around behind the man, to tip him backward, but a rug slipped under his foot and threw him off balance. He fell back upon the bed. But even as he fell he kicked out with his right leg, and his right foot caught the gunman in the most painful place of all.

It was not really a nice thing to do, but who the hell wants to be nice to a murderer?

The Greek screamed. He squeezed the gun twice more as he fell. He got up on one elbow almost instantly, but by that time Morton had rolled backward right over the bed.

The second brother came charging in from the living room, his enormous Colt leveled. Morton ducked. The Colt thundered; and plaster trickled down upon the back of Morton's head and the back of his neck. There was barely room, between the low bed and the wall on that side, for him to lie flat.

The Colt thundered again, then once more.

But this was as nothing compared with the racket McGarvey made. It wasn't much of a door he bucked—

for that matter, this wasn't much of a house—and it went through at the second shoulder-slam falling down flat upon the living room floor with a bang which almost knocked the glass out of the windows.

The man with the Colt turned to meet McGarvey. He was standing almost in the doorway between the two rooms. He made no attempt to hide, but held the gun at full-length in front of him and fired four times.

The gun kicked in his hand, throwing it up, and after the first shot his aim was always a little high.

The man with the Savage was warier. He got to one knee and peered around the edge of the doorway. He swayed dizzily—his temples were greenish, his lips perfectly white—but he raised his pistol deliberately.

MORTON HAD HALF-RISEN. Dizzy too, and almost breathless, he threw himself into a long dive clear over the bed and landed upon the kneeling man's shoulders from behind.

It stunned them both. Morton stirred, tried to raise his head—and then it felt as though the ceiling had fallen on him.

It wasn't the ceiling, however. It was the man who held the Colt.

Young McGarvey, spread-legged in the living room, put two more shots into that man as he lay on the top of the pile. Then he dragged him off, dragged Morton off, and with the heel of his hand smacked the other brother's head twice upon the floor, hard. The other brother, as it happened, was unconscious anyway; but when there wasn't time to find this out, why should McGarvey take any chances? He went to his partner.

"They hurt you, Mort? Did the rats hurt you?"

"I—I don't think so," Morton whispered. He nodded weakly toward the living room. "Another one…. Big fellow…."

"I clouted him. He tried to grab me around the waist."

"I—I guess—he didn't have—gun."

He shook his head, wetted his lips, swallowed. With young McGarvey's assistance he rose. His left hand stung where the hammer of the Savage had bitten into it, and he had a shrieking headache, but otherwise he seemed to be all right.

"How the hell did *you* get here?" he asked.

"I was looking for you, Mort. I got stuck. I just couldn't seem to think of anything else to do. I must be—I guess I must be a lousy detective after all, Mort, the way you've always said."

What a lot this was, coming from young McGarvey!

"So this afternoon I decided I'd better admit I was a damn fool, and go to you and tell you that. And then I couldn't find you! Nobody knew where you were. Well, I was standing around wondering where to start, when a call came in from some Italians that'd just moved into a house in Southwest Twenty-second. They were all het up. Seems they'd had a man there from the light company, and they were suspicious because another man had read their meter only this morning.

"Well, I figured that Italians and Greeks look alike to some people, and maybe you were out this way looking for Greeks, because I knew you sometimes pull that gag about being a meter inspector. So I called the Italians back and asked them to describe the second man better, and they did, and it was you. So I came out here myself and started asking around, and this is the twentieth house I tried."

Morton muttered, "You do get an idea now and then, don't you?" He gazed around. "This baby I jumped"—he pushed the man's head with a stubby, somewhat dusty shoe, and got a groan in response—"is still among us. But not this other baby."

"I shot him three times, to make certain," McGarvey confessed.

"Good idea. These two are brothers, and they were sore at Stanley because he cheated them of their life savings. He'd cheated the other guy at the same time. And then of course he'd skipped. But these babies swore revenge—and they meant it! When they found out somehow that Stanley was down here, they came right along. They meant to hang him, which is why they happened to have that rope. But when they located him he was talking fast and low to a man they recognized from his pictures as Sam T. Packhard, so they figured they might as well make a little jack while they were at it, and instead of going for Stanley then and there they waited till he got back to his apartment. Then they walked in on him. Trying to hold them off, he told them how he'd talked Packhard into a skin game and that Packhard was due soon with a lot of money. So they kept him there. When Packhard did arrive I suppose he didn't like their looks and started to back out, but one of them cracked him in the jaw or something.

"Then they were scared. They knew it wasn't a good thing to smack a multimillionaire, and he'd seen them. So they hauled him into the next apartment—Stanley's key fitted it, the way most of those keys fit most of the locks in that dump—and strung him up. Then they beat it, taking Stanley with them. They took him as far as Bayfront Park, and you know what they did to him there."

"But why in the world should a man like—"

"That's the strangest part. Here was a fellow everybody said was one of the greatest financial wizards that ever lived. He was a genius. He had one of the most brilliant minds of his day. But he never used it for anything except to make more and more and more money; and after a while it began to go soft on him. They said he retired, but it was his brain that retired, not him. They kept him away from the public, and had a bodyguard to watch him night and day; and they were arranging, from what I hear, to have him declared legally insane. But it isn't a cinch to do a thing like that without publicity, and they had to go slow.

"He was harmless. Just a little dotty. He was discussing all sorts of wild money-making schemes, and they were afraid he'd bust out and push down the whole structure.

"How George Stanley happened to get him is something we'll never know. It must have been an accident. Stanley wouldn't have dreamed of going after game one-sixteenth as big as that. But the bodyguard had a habit of parking the old man somewhere and slipping out for a drink, and I suppose during one of those sessions the old man met Stanley, who instinctively went into his act."

"You mean a punk like that took in one of the greatest business minds in history?"

Morton nodded.

"What *had been* one of the greatest minds. And what's more, Stanley was working the oldest and cheapest stunt of them all."

Morton nodded to the wooden box in the corner—the box with the shiny gadgets on top and the rectangle of glass in the side.

"That's what I was looking for. I got a friend in New York on long distance, and he told me about George Stanley. This man's in Centre Street, and guys like Stanley are his specialty. He described this box. Seems they took it away from Stanley a few months ago, but before they had a chance to destroy it damned if a lawyer didn't get a court order and made 'em give it back! So I figured Stanley would still have this box, and that the killers would take it along. He told them he'd fooled Sam T. Packhard with it, and sure enough they saw Packhard and saw his cash. So they figured that if Stanley could make a fortune out of the contraption, why couldn't they? They were dumb like that."

"But what *is* the thing?"

"An old-fashioned money-making machine. I can remember when the country was full of guys selling them. The simplest ones used to be just a box with a crank. You put a roll of paper into one end, and turned the crank, and real dollar bills fell out a slot at the other end. All you needed was some sleight-of-hand ability and a few genuine bills—and good legs for when the sucker finally learned the truth.

"This particular one"—Morton rapped it—"is pretty fancy. It looks like it was one of those where you put the money between two blotters that are supposed to be soaked in some chemical, and then you switch on a couple of dry cells to make a humming, and maybe you spin the dials for a while—and you leave it that way overnight. When you open it up in the presence of the sucker, after a lot more fussing, the money is doubled. The extra, of course, was hidden in a false bottom. A couple of successful trials and the sucker draws everything he's got out of the bank and hands it to you. And you disappear."

McGARVEY WHISPERED, "CRIPES! It's like as if some-body worked the old handkerchief game on J.P. Morgan, or Jesse Livermore lost his dough to a gang of shines using tops-and-bottoms!"

Morton nodded, said:

"Just about like that. Old Packhard had driven himself so hard getting money that his mind went bad, and yet he didn't know how to stop. And there he was, the greatest market rigger since Jay Gould and Daniel Drew, sneaking off like a school kid playing hooky, and handing fifty grand cash to a fourth-rate confidence man."

McGarvey, nervous from embarrassment, avoiding his partner's eye, had found a brown paper package under-neath the coat of the husky man. It looked like a package anybody might carry home from the chain store on the corner. McGarvey snapped the string—and bright new, stiff, noisy banknotes cascaded in a yellow stream to the floor. McGarvey gasped, for he had never before seen so much money. He started to pick it up hurriedly, as though he were afraid it would evaporate.

"So he made so much dough that it drove him off his nut? Well, I guess that's something will never happen to us, Mort."

"I guess so," Morton said.

McGarvey fastened the package, laid it aside.

"You know, Mort. About that business in Monty's office—"

"What business?"

"Well, I mean— Well, about you and me, and all that."

"I don't know what you're talking about," said Morton.

"Okay," said young McGarvey, and his face split in an immense grin.

www.ingramcontent.com/pod-product-compliance
Lightning Source LLC
Chambersburg PA
CBHW030537030726
47495CB00004B/1025